The Long Weekend

Lynn Wyatt

BookLocker

Trenton, Georgia

Paperback ISBN: 978-1-958891-05-6
Hardcover ISBN: 978-1-958891-06-3
Ebook ISBN: 979-8-88531-595-1

Published by BookLocker.com, Inc., Trenton, Georgia.

Printed on acid-free paper.

The characters and events in this book are fictitious. Any similarity to real persons, living or dead, is coincidental and not intended by the author.

BookLocker.com, Inc.
2023

First Edition

Library of Congress Cataloguing in Publication Data
Wyatt, Lynn
The Long Weekend by Lynn Wyatt
Library of Congress Control Number: 2023919302

Book Dedication

Thank you to my wife Mendi for her
encouragement to keep on writing.

Chapter 1
Water Rescue /the Pub

Wednesday
October 24, 1973
Anchorage, Alaska

Jim stepped outside his hangar door to watch three floatplanes taxi across the still water of Lake Hood in single file formation. The two de Havilland DHC-2 Beavers and one Cessna 206, all painted in blue livery and red stripes, belonged to the largest air taxi operator on the lake, famous for their sightseeing flights around Mt. McKinley. Jim expected the planes were full of passengers loaded up with camera gear for their first seaplane ride and flightseeing adventure of the Alaskan wilderness. It looked to him like they intended to make a synchronized takeoff to the east, one behind the other, as an attention grabber for the spectators parked around the lake.

Jim wished he were piloting one of those aircraft instead of watching them, but he was stuck here on the ground working. His own Cessna 185 floated a few yards away, tied to his maintenance dock waiting for an oil change. Summer had faded to fall taking most of the charter season with it, and until business picked up again, his income would rely on servicing and repairing planes rather than flying them. He glanced inside the hangar where his new employee Ronnie King lay under a Twin Otter working on the amphibious floats.

"Going okay?" Jim yelled to be heard over the chattering of Ronnie's rivet gun.

"No problem, Dude. Just about finished."

Jim looked back to watch the three floatplanes glide by, their wakes gently rocked his Cessna. The planes lined up for a take-off to the east, then the one in front accelerated as the pilot applied full power to the big 450 HP radial engine. The floats rose onto the step, planed off while still accelerating, and the craft lifted into the air. The second airplane followed close behind the first. Too close, Jim realized. As it rose, its wings rocked then rolled hard to the left into an almost ninety-degree bank. The left wingtip hit the water, the plane tumbled, and upon impact started to sink.

Jim gaped, momentarily stunned, but recovered almost immediately knowing there would be people trapped inside. "Ronnie! Plane crash, come on!"

The third floatplane pulled up beside the sinking one. The pilot shut down the engine, jumped out, and dived into the water as Jim and Ronnie ran to Jim's floatplane at the dock. They quickly untied it, fired up the engine, and headed out to help. Reaching the crash site Jim shut down the engine and Ronnie dove out the side door into the water. Jim stood on the floats where he grabbed gasping people from the two swimmers, and pulled them to safety, one after another.

A short time later, the Lake Hood rescue boat arrived and with everyone's help, the passengers and their pilot were soon out of the water, wrapped in blankets and on their way back to shore. It appeared all of them had survived the shocking experience without serious injury.

With the rescue complete and the rush of excitement over, Jim and Ronnie taxied back to the dock. While Jim was still mostly dry, soaked Ronnie shivered inside a blanket.

"What do you think went wrong?" Ronnie asked through his clattering teeth.

"Wake turbulence. The second airplane was too close to the first. The Beaver is a heavy airplane and its wings generate wake turbulence after liftoff. With no wind today, the second aircraft flew right into its wake and it rolled him over. It's a good lesson for you to remember, assuming you still want to fly."

"For sure, Dude."

"Good," Jim said, glad to hear it. He'd promised to teach his new apprentice how to fly. "Nice job back there, by the way."

"Thanks. Glad I was there to help, but I'm freezing my butt off now.

"Let's get you dried off and call it quits for the day. We can hit the pub for a few beers on me.

"Sounds great." Ronnie smiled despite his shaking. "Man that water was freaking cold."

***

Entering the Super Cub Pub on the shore of Lake Hood, Jim and Ronnie shed their parkas, hats, and gloves, and hung them on hooks by the door. After Ronnie's heroic performance this afternoon, Jim decided it was time to introduce him to the local bush pilot scene, and this was their favorite drinking hole.

The locals loved this place for its old Alaska style with floor-to-ceiling knotty pine, and a man-sized rock fireplace that always burned bright at the far end. Bear skins and moose heads hung on the walls next to photos of pilots and their airplanes. On one side, a long bar built of stacked logs held a foot-tall jar of pickled eggs, a buck each, and baskets of free peanuts. The wall behind the bar was backed with mirrors and shelves of liquor. Rough-hewn tables filled the center of the room and booths lined the far side.

As always, the place was dimly lit and smelled of burning wood, cigarettes, grilled meat, and spilled beer. There was also the aroma of its customers, bearded men who smelled of sweat, engine oil, campfire smoke, fish, and dirt that came from a long day of hard work. After stopping in here to unwind, most of them would return home to their families for the night before rising early to do it all over again tomorrow.

For newcomers like Ronnie, the sharp odors and rough talk might be unpleasant, but for Jim, it was all comfortably familiar. This was his kind of place, his kind of friends—men who would risk anything to help each other. Like him, they knew every inch of their airplanes, knew how to fix them, and knew how to fly them. These were Alaskan bush pilots, a rare breed, flying into places unthinkable to those in the lower 48, in weather that would keep other pilots grounded, and carrying loads so heavy they had to devise their own tricks just to get airborne. Their job was one of the most dangerous in the world, and every year, they lost friends. Some of those pilot's bodies were eventually found, and some never were, but despite the danger and the losses, the common thread was that they loved what they did and would have it no other way.

Jim nodded at familiar faces and raised two fingers at the waitress. When she smiled and nodded in return he knew two beers were on the way. With Jim in the lead, he and Ronnie headed toward an open booth in the back. Their boots crunched on empty peanut shells carpeting the floor as they went, and they had to stop more than once to exchange greetings and shake hands. Jim embarrassed Ronnie repeatedly by introducing him as the swimmer guy who rescued people today.

"Jesus," Ronnie said when they finally slid into the empty booth. "Do you know everybody in here?"

Jim shrugged. "I'm one of them. After you survive a few years of being a bush pilot, it's like you're comrades in war." He squeezed his considerable bulk between the table and hard wooden bench and tried to find room for his feet and legs without invading Ronnie's space. At six foot three, two hundred fifty pounds, Jim didn't always fit in civilized spaces.

"Hey, Jimmy," the waitress said as she set two frosty mugs of beer and a basket of peanuts on their table.

"Hey, Shirl," Jim replied.

Shirl was young, blonde, and cute by most anyone's definition. Dressed in thigh-hi cutoff jeans, fur-topped ankle boots, and a flannel shirt with the sleeves rolled up and the top buttons undone, she grabbed attention.

"Who's your handsome young friend?" She winked at Ronnie and he immediately flushed.

"This here's Ronnie. He helped rescue those people in the lake today."

"My hero," Shirl said and winked again.

"He's my new mechanic from California, so be nice."

"I'm always nice but watch out for the guys in here. They love to mess with newbies. "You boys want something to eat? We've got salmon and moose burgers on the grill." She winked again.

"No thanks, the wife's expecting me," Ronnie answered.

"Just the beers, Shirl," Jim confirmed reluctantly. He was expected home as well.

"Suit yourselves." She gave them another wink and sashayed away.

Ronnie watched her for a moment. "She always flirt like that?"

It's how she makes her tips. But she doesn't go home with anyone, ever."

"How would you know that?"

Jim smirked. "I've known her since we were kids."

"You've lived in Anchorage your whole life?"

"No. Grew up in a homestead cabin out in the bush. If I had my way, I'd still be out there, but Karen likes city life. She tried living out in my cabin with me for a while, but couldn't handle it, so we moved into town." Jim let out a long sigh and took a swallow of his beer. He glanced around at the other tables, seeing hand-flying gestures as pilots exchanged stories of their latest exploits. It made him itch to get back in the air. He'd spent too much time working on planes lately and not nearly enough time flying.

From across the room, a pair of rheumy blue eyes looked back at him. *Oh, Jeez,* Jim thought and looked away, hoping that would be the end of it. Instead, the old man stood and walked towards them. Jim cursed under his breath.

"Haven't seen you in a while, Jimmy. What you been up to? Mind if I sit a spell? Who's your friend here?" He didn't wait for answers, already lowering himself to take a seat.

Forced to scoot over, Ronnie grimaced and then covered his lower face against the intruder's malodor.

"Ronnie, meet Old Red, the oldest bush pilot in the state," Jim introduced them grudgingly even as his mind raced to come up with a way to get rid of the old man without making a scene.

Few knew how "old" Red really was, but he'd been a town fixture for as long as anyone could remember. Most guesses put him close to ninety. Though once famous for being an excellent pilot and big game guide, he hadn't aged well and was now known as the town drunk. Most people blamed Red's decline on the death of his wife. If Red ever bathed it wasn't evident and his appearance never varied—long greasy gray hair and beard, dirty dark flannel pants with red suspenders worn over ragged long johns soiled to the point that their original color was barely discernable—white maybe? A navy-blue baseball cap with 'Old Red' embroidered in scarlet never left his head. His florid cheeks and bleary eyes testified that he already had a few beers under his belt, and no doubt was hoping for more at Jim's expense—not that he'd get any.

"Yep, I been flying up here going on some seventy years now. Got the best bush plane in the business." Red grinned revealing missing teeth.

"You still fly?" Ronnie asked, dropping his hand in disbelief.

"Ain't nobody stopped me yet, and sure as hell better not try." Red squinted at the young man next to him, taking in the long blond ponytail and the blue T-shirt with a surfer riding a huge cresting wave below the word 'Cowabunga!' emblazoned across the chest. "Where you from, boy?"

"California. Manhattan Beach. Just moved up here."

"A *Cheechako* then."

"A what?"

"You fly?"

"No, but I'd like to learn. Jim's offered to give me lessons."

"Has he now? Well, you lucked out there. I taught his dad all about flying and surviving out in the bush, and he taught Jimmy here, but till he teaches you, best stay close to town. Out there's wild country and it don't cotton to fools that think they know how to fly."

"I'm no fool," Ronnie countered and narrowed his eyes in return.

Red snorted a laugh. "Now don't be getting' your knickers all in a bunch. Meant no disrespect. You're a newbie is all, a Cheechako. I been here all my life and even I'm still learnin'. Trust me, Alaska's like nothing you've ever experienced."

"Sounds like you might have some interesting stories," Ronnie said.

"Stories? Ha! Oh, have I got stories. Close calls and closer ones. Fish as big as you and bears twice as tall."

Ronnie laughed. "I'd like to see any fish as big as me."

"You'd have to know where to find 'em." Red bobbed his bushy gray eyebrows and grinned slyly. "I have a secret place."

"Really?" Ronnie's eyes widened, apparently open to hearing some tall tale he might or might not believe.

Alaska was full of stories and 'Old Red' loved to tell them, but Jim wasn't in the mood. "Don't encourage him."

"Hold on, boy. Even you don't know about this lake of mine," Red said.

"Think I've seen most every lake within range."

"Not this one. It's way out in the Talkeetna Mountain range, deep in those winding canyons—real hard to find and treacherous. I wouldn't trust most pilots, but if you're good enough, it's worth it … pure magic. You have to turn your back when baiting your hook or the fish jump right out to bite it." He snapped his fingers in illustration. "There's lake trout over a hundred pounds in there."

"That so?" Jim was skeptical but intrigued despite himself.

Ronnie looked at Jim. "Hey, you have been promising to show me the backcountry and do some fishing. Maybe this is what we've been waiting for."

Red scratched his chin through his dirty beard. "Well, I don't know. If I was of a mind to share with anyone, it'd be my boy Jimmy here, but you're just a Cheechako." Red leaned back and crossed his arms.

Jim decided to call his bluff. "Ronnie, would you mind going out to my truck and getting my flight bag?"

"Here, lemme get out of your way." Red stood from the table and waited for Ronnie to move.

Ronnie looked from one man to the other, nonplussed, but the message was clear. They wanted him gone. "Fine." He scooted out the end of the bench.

"I need a sectional chart," Jim added in explanation.

"Yeah, sure." Ronnie frowned and headed toward the front door.

Red squinted at Ronnie's back as he walked away. "You trust that kid?"

"I do. He might look like a brainless surfer, but he's got his shit together. So what's all this about a secret lake, or are you just messing with a Cheechako?"

Red sat back down. "No, it's real alright. Truth is I been feelin' my years of late and don't know how many I got left in me. Think it's time to pass on a few of my secrets." He grabbed Ronnie's beer and slurped it before Jim could intervene. Red sighed and his eyes stared off to some faraway place. "Never know when the end's-comin', now do ya? I been thinkin' on things, mistakes I've made. I'd like to bury some of those old hurts before it's time to bury me."

Jim frowned, uncomfortable with the turn of conversation, and was more than relieved to have it cut short by Ronnie's return. He dropped Jim's flight bag heavily on the table and asked in an annoyed tone, "So should I make myself scarce again?"

"Naw. Jimmy here says you're okay." Red slid over and patted the bench for Ronnie to sit.

"Thanks, I guess." Ronnie sat, then scowled seeing that his beer was now firmly in Red's grip.

Jim thumbed through the bag and pulled out a sectional chart. He handed it over to Red along with a red-inked pen from his shirt pocket. "Show me."

"Happy to." Red refolded the chart to frame the Talkeetna mountain section then leaned over it with one arm wrapped around the map to block anyone's view but theirs.

"Here's Talkeetna." Red circled the town and then drew a dotted line upwards. "Fly north about 40 miles to where the Susitna River flows out of a canyon on your right. If you get to Chulitna, you missed it. Follow it upriver for about 30 miles. When it makes a sharp turn to the right keep on goin' straight until you see another river flowin' out on your left. Turn there and fly up Deadman Creek for another 15 miles. Starts gettin' pretty narrow, but you can get through. The lake's only a few miles more up the canyon, which puts you about 10 miles south of Deadman Mountain." He marked the spot with an X. "Elevation's about 4,000 feet if I remember right and surrounded with tall mountains. Ignore all these other lakes marked on your chart here, it's none of them. You won't spot mine until you're nearly on top of it. Like I said, it's a bit tricky gettin' in and out, but you should be fine. You'll know my lake when you see it. At one end is a beautiful sandy white beach and a wide meadow climbin' up the foot of the mountain. Make sure you have full tanks before you go. You might even take a couple extra cans. I almost ran dry coming back the first time."

Jim squinted at the red X marked where the map showed nothing but mountains. "You sure this lake exists, or did you just dream it while you were drunk?"

"Don't be like that, boy. Give me the benefit of the doubt for once." Red shoved the chart across the table. "It's there I tell you but do what you like. Just don't go blabbin' about it. If the damned tourists ever find out, it'll get ruined."

Jim turned the chart around to examine the route more closely. Red's dotted red line led through familiar landmarks and beyond. Like Red said, it was a long way out, which was exactly where he longed to be. It sounded perfect, maybe too perfect, which made him even more suspicious and wanting even more now to know whether Red was being truthful. He hadn't always been. The two of them shared a complicated history, one Jim didn't discuss with anyone, not even his wife.

Jim sat there studying the map, considering the pros and cons. Though late in the season, there should still be a few weeks of good float-flying weather left. Light snow flurries occasionally fluttered in the air, and the snow dusting the mountain tops was creeping inexorably lower each day—'termination dust' as the miners called it—alerting all that it was nearly time to pack up before being frozen in for the winter. Soon the float planes would be pulled off the lake and converted to wheels or skis, but for now, Jim's plane still floated on Lake Hood unhindered by ice.

This time of year, just before winter, was his favorite. The crisp air was too cold for mosquitos, and blueberries covered the hillsides so thick you could fill a five-gallon bucket in minutes. Even fish seemed easier to catch, no doubt eager to fill their bellies before winter set in. It was at this time of year that the Alaskan bush called to him most strongly, like something primeval in his genes.

"Why not?" His decision made, Jim looked at Ronnie. "You up for a fly-in fishing trip?"

Ronnie smiled and answered. "You bet. Count me in."

Red hooted and slapped the tabletop. "Best goddamn fishing spot in the whole goddamn world. You boys won't regret it or I ain't Old Red."

Seeing his glee Jim and Ronnie both laughed, but in the back of Jim's mind, he reminded himself that 'Old Red' was just a nickname, not this man's true identity.

Chapter 2
Leaving town

Friday, October 26, 1973

It was seven in the morning and the sun wouldn't show up until 9:30. Jim was already awake, dressed, and in his garage gathering supplies. He dragged out his long bag of fishing gear from behind a pile of yard equipment and tools. He batted the bag to knock off the dust from months of neglect. Still in her bathrobe, Karen leaned her shoulder against the door connecting the garage to their house, holding it open while drinking a coffee as she watched him loading supplies into the back of his pickup.

Jim walked over to her, gave her a hug and a pat on the butt. "Fishing season's almost over. If I don't go now, I'll miss it altogether. I don't want to let it slip by without taking at least one good trip."

"It will do you good, you've been working some long hours and I want you to get away. I have lots to keep me busy.

"So where exactly is this so-called secret lake? "Karen asked."

"Up in the Talkeetna Mountains. Old Red drew me a map. Said the fishing's amazing. Sounded too good to pass up."

"So let me get this straight. You're flying off to look for some secret lake in the backcountry based on a map drawn by the town drunk? Sounds kind of crazy to me but I know you guys will have a good time."

"Even if we can't find old Reds lake there are plenty of other lakes in the area. I checked the weather. It should hold."

"And you're taking that new guy you hired with you? The one you call 'the surfer dude'?

"Yea, Ronnie, this is a big adventure for him, and I enjoy his company."

"I'm going to miss you, but it's only for a few days."

Jim took a long look at his wife....fifteen years of marriage hadn't changed her much. Her hair was still a long dark red, her blue eyes might have creases in their corners now, but the way they sparkled when she laughed or saw something no one else did still made him blink in surprise.

Giving her a quick kiss he slung the fishing gear into the back of his truck alongside the packed food and camping equipment fired up the truck and pulled out.

Their pine-sided house with all its daily demands receded in the rearview mirror, and the open road and star-speckled indigo sky beckoned ahead.

***

When Jim reached Ronnie's dark residential street, he saw his friend standing at the edge of his front yard bundled in a heavy parka. An overstuffed three-foot-long canvas bag sat on the ground. Jim pulled his truck to a stop and nodded at him out the driver's window.

"By the looks of that pack, you brought everything I told you and then some."

"Yep, got it all, plus Pattie's home-baked cookies and some other stuff she insisted I take." Ronnie turned and waved toward his house. A hand on the other side of the window waved back.

"Is she okay with you going?" Jim asked, squinting at the shadowy form inside. He'd never met Pattie, but Ronnie bragged about her a lot.

"Sure. She got excited when I told her we were following a hand-drawn map to a secret lake way back in the Talkeetna Mountains. It's like a treasure hunt. I promised to bring her back a bunch of fish. She plans to give your wife a call today if that's okay. They'll probably party the whole time we're gone."

"Great idea, hope they hit it off" From the driver's seat, he pointed at the bulging pack on the ground. "Need help with that?"

"No, dude, I got it." With a grunt of effort, Ronnie slung the pack into the back of the pick-up, then ran around and climbed into the passenger seat. As soon as he closed the door, Jim hit the gas, eager to get on the road. A large white dog ran alongside barking until Ronnie stuck his head out the window and yelled, "Go home, Leroy

"He yours?" Jim asked as

"Nope, our neighbor's. They let him stay outside most of the time. Me and Leroy have become good buddies. He loves to play ball and I keep dog biscuits for him."

"What's the latest weather forecast?" Ronnie asked.

"All good as of this morning. Clear skies, moderate winds, slight chance of snow flurries in the higher elevations, but nothing heavy is expected until next week, and we'll be home long before then. We'll take off at about 9:30, right at sunrise.

Sunset's not until 6:30, so that should give us plenty of time to find this secret lake, assuming it's there, of course."

"What if it's not?"

Jim shrugged. "There's plenty more remote lakes back in those mountains. We'll just find one that looks good to us and set down there instead."

They drove along the shoreline of Lake Hood and parked in front of Jim's slip where his Cessna 185 was tied. In the yellow of the truck's headlights, the plane's stripes and numbers looked red, but maroon was the official color. He hated the color and thought often of having the plane repainted, but always talked himself out of doing it as being an unnecessary expense. Karen thought Maroon was pretty. *She'd probably like to paint flowers on it.* The sun had yet to crest the mountains which cast long dark blue shadows across the water and the airplanes silently lining the shore. With winter on the way, the planes would soon have to either come off the lake for parking or be fitted with skis and tied down on the lake ice. Jim threw open his door and took a deep breath of the cool crisp air scented with pine and lake moss. The sky was still a star-bitten black above him, but along the horizon, it was starting to lighten to shades of deep lavender and pink. The sun would soon rise above the mountaintops and brighten the sky to an icy blue, but even now there was light enough to see, so he shut off the headlights and got out. Ronnie did the same and walked over to stand beside him as they looked out across the lake.

"This will probably be my last float-plane flight this year," Jim said, thinking out loud. "Always makes me a little sad."

"I'm looking forward to winter, seeing what it's like. I've never lived anywhere with snow before."

Jim shook his head in amazement that anyone could grow to manhood without experiencing the hard lessons of winter. Ronnie was a Cheechako in the truest sense of the word.

"Do we need to fuel up?" Ronnie asked.

"No, I topped it off yesterday after work and sumped the tanks. The airplane has long-range tanks and I also stowed two extra gas cans in the float compartments, so we've got plenty of fuel to get wherever we're going and back again. I'll open up the plane while you unload the truck, and then you can start handing it over to me. I removed the rear seats to make more room."

"Okay, I'll grab our stuff."

As Ronnie went to unload their gear, Jim stepped onto the plane's left float, sending ripples across the calm waters. He opened up the back cargo door and waited as Ronnie hoisted heavy bags from the truck and carried them over. Jim mentally ticked off the list of supplies as they were loaded …tent, sleeping bags, fishing gear, Coleman lantern, one case of beer, a fifth of Jack Daniels, firewood, food for three days, plus mandatory survival gear which included a 12-gauge shotgun and the 44-magnum pistol Jim carried in a chest holster whenever he flew out. Both men had heavy winter parkas, knit caps, thick wool pants, and Sorel winter boots. Late autumn could get cold.

"Did you file a flight plan?" Ronnie asked.

Jim shook his head. "No point, seeing as our destination's a secret, and we're not exactly sure where we're going."

Ronnie paused. "Does that worry you?"

"No, I hardly ever bother with flight plans anyway. We have the sectional chart Red marked up and I know the area. We'll be fine." He closed up the cargo door. "That's the last of it. You good to go?"

"Hell, yes, dude. Let's get this bird in the air!"

"I hear that, but since you keep telling me you want to learn how to fly, how about if I give you your first lesson—the preflight check."

Jim opened the access panel on top of the float he was standing on and removed a two-foot-long cylindrical water pump. "The first thing is pumping out all the float compartments to get rid of accumulated water." He handed Ronnie the pump. "Everywhere you see a cap, remove it and start pumping until no water flows. It should be pretty dry, but we have to make sure."

"Got it," Ronnie took over the pumping operation.

Jim supervised until satisfied all the float compartments were dry. "Good. Next, we do the walk-around." Ronnie followed him. "It's the same thing as you do as a mechanic, check the fuel and oil levels, and inspect all the control surfaces for damage—water rudders and cables, prop and cowlings, struts and float attachments."

Together they examined each item.

"Everything looks good to me. Agreed?" Jim waited for Ronnie's nod. "Okay, let's untie and climb aboard."

Jim opened the left-hand door and climbed into the pilot seat. Ronnie climbed in through the right-hand door to the co-pilot seat. Both positions had full flight controls

"Remember, hands-off, unless I say so. Understood?"

"Got it."

They fastened their seat belts, secured the doors, and put on their headsets. Jim pulled out a list from the door compartment.

"Remember, even if you think you know this stuff like the back of your hand, still use the checklist to make sure you don't forget anything." He handed the list to Ronnie. "Read it off to me, line-by-line."

Ronnie read and waited for Jim's confirmation for each item. "Preflight, seatbelts, fuel shutoff valve …"

Jim checked each item until the list was complete. "Okay, now the engine-start checklist. Mixture rich, prop high RPM, master switch on, fuel pump on two seconds then off, throttle closed, prop clear, ignition start." The 300 HP engine roared to life, a sound Jim loved. "After starting, oil pressure check. Radio master on."

"Radio check, you hear me ok?" Jim asked.

"Loud and clear," Ronnie responded.

"Okay, here we go."

"Lake Hood tower, Cessna N5416R at southeast tie-down, request clearance to taxi for an east take-off."

The tower voice replied, "Roger Cessna 5416R. Winds calm. Altimeter 29.89. Cleared to taxi for an east take-off,"

"16R cleared to taxi," Jim added a bit of power and the airplane slid from the bank. He lowered the water rudders and turned to the west, slow taxing with idle power as the engine warmed up.

The water was smooth as glass, their airplane creating a slight wake that rocked the sleeping airplanes along the shoreline. They were the only airplane out this early.

"Okay, now that the oil temp has warmed up a bit, we can do our before-takeoff checks and run-up." Ronnie watched closely as Jim performed each task while the plane continued to taxi.

"We'll use one notch of flaps for takeoff," Jim said as he pulled the flap handle up to the first detent. "And don't let me forget to raise the water rudders before takeoff. It will cost me a case of beer if I forget and one of my buddies catches me." Reaching the west end of the lake Jim turned the airplane to face east. Ronnie shadowed his eyes against the sun as it peaked over the mountaintops and reflected off the water.

Jim pressed the mike button on the control yoke again. "Lake hood tower 16R ready for takeoff east request northbound departure."

"N5416R cleared for takeoff east, northbound departure approved, have a nice day" came the tower's reply.

"16R cleared for takeoff east, nice day to you too," Jim answered.

Jim retracted the water rudders and then slowly pushed the throttle to max power holding the control wheel full aft. The big engine roared as the plane accelerated. As the front of the floats started to lift Jim gently eased the control wheel forward to level the airplane onto the step. The plane raced down the lake like a speedboat, accelerating and growing lighter. Reaching sixty knots airspeed, Jim reached down and slightly rotated the trim wheel aft and they gently lifted into the air.

Jim slowly lowered the flap handle to retract the flaps, pulled back the throttle to 25 inches of manifold pressure and the prop to 2500 RPM, climb power setting.

"Woohoo!" Ronnie yelled. "Look out fish! Here we come."

Jim grinned at Ronnie's enthusiasm but kept his mind on flying the plane. Already passing through seven hundred feet altitude, he turned north and kept climbing up to 9,500 feet. A safe altitude for flying over the mountainous terrain ahead. The Chugach Mountains surrounding them were lighting up like diamonds from the snow-capped peaks in the early morning sun. The turnoff to Red's secret lake in the Talkeetna Mountains lies 130 miles north. He aimed the nose at the tallest point— Mount McKinley—known as Denali (the great one) to the indigenous population. Its jagged peak rose in the distance, a majestic sentinel, a snow-topped purple colossus to guide them on their journey. Jim adjusted the power settings to cruise and leaned the mixture control, trimmed the airplane for level flight, and told Ronnie he could fly the airplane while he kicked back to enjoy the flight. "Just keep us pointed at McKinley and try to keep us at this altitude. It'll be good practice for you." Jim stated.

"Okay man, I got this baby under control." Said Ronnie enthusiastically and he took the controls with a smile on his face.

Chapter 3
The Secret Lake

Friday, October 26, 1973

Rugged wilderness passed beneath the plane as Ronnie flew north from Lake Hood while Jim supervised and watched for the first landmark on their route. When he spotted red rooftops flanking a road below, he pointed them out.

"That's Talkeetna. We have to fly north another forty miles then look for the Susitna River.

"Right. I remember Red saying if we get to Chulitna we've gone too far."

"Okay, Ronnie, Time to switch! I have the controls," Jim said as he placed his hands on the yoke.

"You got it, Captain." Ronnie let go and leaned back.

Jim handed him the map with Red's hand-marked route to his secret lake. "Follow us on the sectional chart and help me look for landmarks." Jim pushed in the mixture, eased back the power, and lowered the nose, starting a gradual descent to a lower altitude.

Fifteen minutes later, Ronnie pointed toward long ribbons of muddy brown. "Hey, I think that's it, the Susitna River."

"Yep, that looks like it." Jim leveled off to about 1000 feet above the terrain then banked to the right to line up with the river. "We're supposed to follow the river for about thirty miles then look for where it makes a sharp turn to the right."

"Right," Ronnie confirmed looking at the map. A few minutes later he shouted, "Look. There's the turn—just like on the chart."

"Okay good, we're getting close. Do you see Deadman Creek on the chart?"

"Yeah, got it. That's where we're supposed to turn."

"Okay good. So now we're looking for a river that flows out from our left then follow it in. I'm going to slow down to enter those canyons." Jim lowered the flaps one notch "No telling what we're going to find."

"Good idea. Oh, I see it. There," Ronnie said and pointed to a crooked ribbon of muddy brown coming up on their left.

"That's it." Jim pulled back the power, pushed in the prop control, to slow to eighty knots, and then made a gentle controlled turn to follow this new river into the narrow canyon named Deadman Creek. Tall granite walls scaled both sides of them now with barely enough room to circle back.

"Man, I see why more people don't fly through here, this is scary tight," said Ronnie.

"We're fine. Should be seeing the lake soon, if we're in the right place." Jim tightened his grip on the control wheel as they rounded the next corner, prepared to react quickly should this canyon suddenly end. The bend tightened into an unnerving blind with no room to maneuver. Jim prepared to hit full power and climb free, but then the narrow canyon broke out into a wide valley surrounded by towering white-capped mountains. Directly ahead lay a crystal-blue lake about three hundred yards long and a hundred yards wide, glittering under the sun like a polished gem. Jim exhaled.

"This is it, Dude. We found it." Ronnie punched his fist in the air. "Man, I can't wait to get a line in that water."

Here above the tree line, only bare rocky granite cliffs and boulders encircled the lake except on the north end where a sandy beach fronted a wide meadow. What looked like a large brown patch in the meadow's center was surrounded by rolling red, orange, and yellow tundra that crawled partway up the rocky cliffs.

"Yeah, looks good. Okay, follow along with me as we land." Ronnie gave him a thumbs up. Jim performed the pre-landing checklist quickly, knowing that with his mechanic background, Ronnie would grasp it.

"GUMP is our abbreviated checklist. G-gas on both tanks, U-undercarriage, doesn't apply to straight floats, M-mixture, full rich or as required, P-prop, set to climb power. Got it?"

"Got it."

Circling the lake, Jim aimed into the wind, lowered the flaps to forty degrees, and slowed to sixty-five knots, describing each action out loud for Ronnie's benefit as they descended. "Raise the nose a bit and apply a touch of power to let the floats gently touch down."

The plane settled onto the water with barely a ripple.

"Then ease it back to let the airplane fall off the step before lowering the water rudders. There." When the nose leveled, he slowly taxied to thirty feet off the beach then shut the engine down to let the plane's momentum carry them the rest of the way.

"We can do the shutdown checklist while we're still moving. Mixture? Cutoff. Mags? Off. Master switch? Off.

Radio master? Off. Shutdown check complete. And that's how you do it." Jim concluded the landing lesson just as the front of the floats gently slid onto the sand.

What from the sky had looked like a brown patch suddenly came alive. Hundreds of eyes, ears, and antlers appeared in the meadow as a herd of grazing caribou raised their heads. The closest caribou sprinted away, spooking more of them. Finally, the least alarmed members of the herd followed the others at a leisurely pace. Once satisfactorily distanced from the intrusion, the caribou went back to grazing.

"Wow! I didn't even see them until they moved." Ronnie opened the door and raised his arms as if aiming. "If I had my rifle, I could get us one for dinner."

"Don't bother. Caribou's too big to eat on a weekend and the seasons is over now so we can't take it back with us. Besides, we brought T-bone steaks, remember?" Then Jim spotted something on the beach that surprised him more than the caribou. "Well now, would you look at that? Someone's gone and dug us a fire pit and left us a big pile of wood."

"Must have been Old Red," Ronnie said. "We'll have to say thanks when we get back."

"Let's get moving. We need to secure the airplane and set up camp so we can cook dinner before dark. And maybe catch some fish to go with those T-bones."

"Right on, Dude."

They climbed out onto the floats and jumped down on the sand. The priority was to tie the plane down by running lines from the front float cleats to stakes in the ground. Within thirty minutes they had the plane secured, their gear unloaded, their two-man tent set up, and the fire pit and grill readied to cook dinner.

"I can't wait any longer," Ronnie said and grabbed his fishing gear. "Time to fish."

"Be right there," Jim said but was still puttering around camp when Ronnie yelled. "Yahoo! Got one. Don't know what it is yet, but it's putting up a hell of a fight."

Jim paused to watch Ronnie drag in a monster Arctic Grayling, a freshwater cousin of salmon, and probably the biggest one Jim had ever seen. He walked over to admire it.

"Wow, that's a real beauty—what are you using for bait?"

"A pixie lure," Ronnie said and wiggled the hot pink fish shape for Jim to see before casting his line back into the water. "The guy at the sporting goods store said it's the latest and greatest. I guess he knew his stuff because they're all over it. Looks like Red was right too, I mean about this place."

"So it would seem," He hurried back to grab his gear as Ronnie caught a second grayling before Jim even got his line in the water, but minutes later a fish grabbed hold. He let it run, then started working it back to shore. The scales of another huge grayling flashed rainbow hues in the sun as he pulled it from the water. "I think this guy's even bigger than yours."

"Not for long." Ronnie threw his lure back into the water.

They couldn't keep them off. Cast and catch, over and over, more fish than they could ever eat, but the fun now was in the catch and release. The two of them laughed like kids, comparing the sizes of their graylings before throwing the smaller ones back. They settled on keeping the four biggest ones—real trophy winners if anyone had been judging a contest. Ronnie ran for his camera and insisted Jim take a picture as he grabbed two of the biggest fish by their gills and lifted them shoulder-high on either side. Their tails reached past his knees.

"I bet no one's fished this lake in years," Jim said as he squinted through the camera window to square Ronnie in the shot.

"Yeah, no one but Old Red, and us now."

"Smile." He clicked the camera, then advanced the 35 mm film for the next shot.

"You sure you got it? No one's going to believe how big these are unless I have proof."

"I got it, trust me."

"Okay, thanks." Ronnie set the fish down and took the camera back. "Want me to take a picture of you?"

Jim shook his head. "Naw, don't waste your film. Come on, let's get these bad boys on the grill."

By the time they finished gorging on fish and steak, the sun had dipped behind the mountains. Seated in their camp chairs, the two men watched the changing colors as the sun set. Ronnie pulled his jacket collar high against the dropping temperature as the light faded. Jim noted an unexpected bite in the air, tossed another log on the campfire, and scowled at the sky. He always kept a close watch on the weather. No sign of clouds, just clear sky from one end of the box canyon to the other, and according to this morning's weather report, it was supposed to remain that way for the next few days, but he also knew that weather prediction was mostly a game of guesswork up here in Alaska where nature could change its mind with little notice.

To shake off his foreboding, he took a deep breath of the clean mountain air, savoring it.

"How about a little nip of the Jack?" Ronnie asked. When Jim nodded, he pulled out the bottle they'd brought. He sank back into his camp chair, opened the lid, and took a swig, before handing it to Jim. "Wow. Got to say it doesn't get any better than this."

"The drink or the view?" Jim took a swallow and passed it back.

"Both!"

They continued passing the whiskey, enjoying the warmth of the campfire and the changing scenery surrounding them. As the sun's glow faded, the towering mountains cast ever longer shadows, and their rocky faces went from maroon to deep purple in the alpenglow, and finally darkened to almost black until their snow-white tops were barely visible. The only sounds were the crackling fire and soft lapping of the water along the edge of the lake. Stars gradually appeared, brightening and multiplying until numerous beyond count or comprehension. The entire firmament was filled with brilliant white dots against a velvet black. Ronnie laughed and pointed at a bright streak zipping across the sky. More shooting stars followed, then suddenly the night lit up with an undulating tapestry of reds, greens, purples, and pinks. Bursts of multicolored lights rippled and swayed above them like a living curtain.

"Whoa," Ronnie whispered. "Far out."

Jim smiled at the look of wonder on Ronnie's face. "The Northern Lights in all their glory. Never seen 'em before?"

Ronnie shook his head without looking away. "I've seen pictures, but … man, they don't do it justice, not even close. All this makes me feel so— I don't know—insignificant, I guess. I've never been religious, but being out here, seeing this. It's so huge—there's no end, no beginning, and it's all so beautiful, so perfect. How could it be just an accident? It had to have been created, right?"

"Maybe. Or maybe it will all be explained someday. Like these lights for instance. What you're seeing, Aurora Borealis is an atmospheric phenomenon caused by solar activity."

"Thanks, Dude, way to ruin a moment. I was talking about miracles."

"So am I, *Dude.* You're looking at charged particles that have traveled 93 million miles from the sun to mingle with atoms in our atmosphere. That's what creates this dazzling light show. Ought to be miraculous enough for anybody."

Ronnie grunted and fingered the tiny St Christopher medal he always wore around his neck—the patron saint for surfers. "I guess. Whether it's scientific or God-given, it's still freaking amazing."

"My point, exactly." They sat around the campfire watching the lights dance for another twenty minutes, each man quiet in his thoughts, mesmerized by the beauty above.

Then the display in the night sky vanished as abruptly as it appeared. They sighed in unison and clapped briefly as if it were the end of a great play or concert.

The full moon rose over the mountains and cast a subtle glow that lit up the landscape and reflected off the white snowcapped mountains. A shiver of pleasure ran down Jim's spine as a lone wolf howled in the distance. He felt as if he'd come home. "God, I love it out here!"

"Yeah. It's like sitting in a giant amphitheater watching nature perform," Ronnie said. "Got to feel sorry for people who never get to experience this."

Jim nodded in agreement. "Great way to finish off the summer."

"Yeah, for sure."

"Well, think I'll call it a night." Jim pushed himself up from his camp chair and stretched his back. "That kind of flying takes it out of you. Wasn't sure about coming way out here on what could have been a wild goose chase, but it all turned out okay."

"Yeah, I'm really glad we didn't crash in that canyon. Not that I ever doubted your piloting skills, boss."

Jim looked at Ronnie sideways, wondering if he was being sarcastic. "Good to know." He yawned. "You staying up?"

"Yeah, I'm not ready to let all this go yet. Think I'll have another sip of the Jack and maybe a toke of my prime homegrown. I expect the girls are having fun tonight too, but no way could it compare to this."

Jim left Ronnie to enjoy the night. He was tired and had seen the starlit skies of Alaska's bush country more times than he could number, but he appreciated what it must be like to see them for the first time. Mindboggling!

Jim crawled into his sleeping bag inside their two-man tent and fell asleep almost as soon as his eyes closed. Ronnie stumbled in a couple of hours later and accidentally stepped on Jim's leg.

"Sorry, man, sorry."

Jim grunted, rolled over, and immediately went back to sleep. It took a lot to rob Jim of his nightly slumber, but an hour later his eyes opened to darkness and the feeling something was wrong. The air inside the tent was too cold and the walls flapped in the wind. He looked over at Ronnie, buried deep in his bag, snoring peacefully. Without disturbing him, Jim climbed out of his bag and unzipped the tent opening to peek outside. His eyes widened.

"Holy shit!" he hissed.

What he saw spooked him the same way they'd startled the caribou, except there was nowhere to run. Before him lay a frozen white landscape of blowing snow. Over a foot of it on the ground already. He hurriedly zipped the opening shut against the wind. He needed to check on the plane, but hesitated for a moment, debating whether to wake Ronnie. He decided against it. There was nothing Ronnie could do for the moment except worry.

Quietly but quickly, Jim slipped into his clothes, grabbed a flashlight, unzipped the tent again, and went out, zipping it shut behind him. To his relief, he found the plane was still tied down despite being bounced around by the wind and the cresting whitecaps hitting the back of the floats. He rechecked each tie to be sure it wouldn't break free then got inside the plane and installed the gust lock, pinning it through the hole in the flight control yoke. Through the windshield, he saw the yellow glare of his flashlight reflecting off ice crystals at the edge of the water, a bad sign. He got out, closed up the plane again, and swept the beam up and down the shoreline, seeing ice forming along the entire length, a *very* bad sign.

Well, hell! It's too early for a winter freeze and the forecast never called for anything like this. Better be a quick storm that blows through or we'll need to get out of here. Either way, we can't do anything until the morning.

He frowned and shook his head. With no option, he returned to the tent and crawled inside to get warm again and try to go back to sleep. There was nothing to do now but wait for first light and sleep was the best way to get there, but for a long time before sleep claimed him again, he listened to Ronnie snore and the wind moan, picturing snow building up all around them and ice growing on the lake.

Chapter 4
Still snowing

Saturday, October 27, 1973

Anchorage.

Karen wandered out to the kitchen, rubbing her forehead to relieve a headache from the too many glasses of wine she and Pattie had consumed with dinner last night. To her surprise, Ronnie's wife Pattie had called her yesterday and invited her out to dinner. She'd wanted to hear all about living in Anchorage, a small town, surrounded by wilderness, and with wild animals wandering the streets downtown. It was all so new to both of them, living in the last frontier. First time away from southern California and it was all a bit frightening to them. Pattie was also worried about Ronnie flying out in the backcountry.

Karen tried to assure Pattie she had nothing to worry about. Jim had been bush-flying up here for many years, and he was one of the best. But underneath, she felt uneasy about their husbands being out this late in the season but stopped herself from sharing that worry with Pattie. They had a great dinner shared a few laughs, and had a few too many glasses of wine

She started the coffee pot and flipped on the TV just as the weather report came on.

"An extreme low-pressure system unexpectedly moved into the area last night bringing freezing temperatures and heavy snowfall into the higher elevations. Travel advisories have been issued and all flights north of Anchorage have been canceled. The storm is expected to last several more days."

Oh no, the guys are out there in the middle of it.

Her phone rang and she picked it up.

"Karen, its Pattie. Have you heard about the storm up north of us? Do you think our guys are in trouble? What do you think we should do?"

Karen knew there was nothing anyone could do in the middle of a storm. The best thing now was to reassure Pattie. "Don't worry. Jim's a good pilot and won't do anything dangerous. They'll probably just weather in for a few days. I'm sure they have everything they need, food, and survival gear, so they should be fine. They'll just have to wait out the storm."

"Does that mean they won't be back on Monday?"

"Hard to say. We'll have to wait and see what the weather does, just like they will."

***

Ronnie woke with a pounding in his head, *a little too much of the Jack last night.* Moving seemed like a really bad idea, but his bladder insisted on it. He had to take a leak—now. No sun lit up the sides of the tent, so he assumed it was still night, but when he looked over at Jim's sleeping bag he saw it was empty which meant Jim was already up, doing something. Ronnie decided he'd better get up too, both to take a pee and to make sure Jim didn't think he was a slacker. He hurriedly pulled on his pants, boots, and jacket, unzipped the tent, and fell face-first into two feet of snow. He clambered up to stand on top of the white ledge around their tent and looked around at the dark grey skies in shock.

"Morning, sleeping beauty," Jim greeted him from several feet away, next to a burning fire.

"What the hell happened?"

"It snowed. We sometimes get that here in Alaska."

"Funny." Ronnie spun in place to look about, eyes wide. "Jesus, I can't even see the top of the mountains. And it's freaking cold."

Jim stoked the fire pit with a long metal prod then added another log. "You might try coming over by the fire."

Ronnie plowed through the knee-deep white powder until he stood next to Jim. He held out his bare hands to warm them over the flames. "Be straight with me, man. Are we in deep shit?"

"No, just snow!"

Ronnie scowled at him. "The more jokes you make, the more you worry me. We can't take off in this, can we?" It was more of a conclusion than a question.

"No, not until it clears up. We'll just watch for a while, and see what the trend is. There's no radio reception, so no weather reports. We'll have to judge things for ourselves. Don't worry, I've been in plenty of bad weather before. I checked the airplane altimeter earlier and the pressure dropped along with the temperature. My biggest concern is the lake could freeze up and trap the plane."

"What?" Ronnie's exclamation sent a cloud of white mist into the freezing air. "You tell me not to worry, then say we might get frozen in?"

"We're not going to let that happen. And even if we did get stuck here for a few days, thanks to Old Red we've got plenty of firewood. With the fish, we've got several days' worth of food to eat, plus we've got our survival gear. We'll be fine."

"You sure about that? I need to take a leak, but it's so freaking cold I don't think I can even find my pecker."

"Get closer to the fire. Just don't piss on it."

Ronnie rolled his eyes and struggled with near-frozen fingers, to get his zipper down. He turned a bit to miss the flames and give himself a modicum of privacy. Finally, he exhaled in relief. "Oh man, I should have stayed in California. I could be hitting the surf right about now."

"Yeah, but then you wouldn't have anything to brag about, would you? Like that light show you saw last night and the giant fish we caught yesterday. Look, I know this isn't much fun right now, but trust me, I've been through plenty worse and come out fine."

Ronnie hurriedly zipped up again, wrapped his arms around himself, and tucked his hands under his armpits. "I sure hope so, dude, cause I am way out of my element."

***

Sunday, October 28, 1973

"Wishing you all a good Sunday morning, this is KTVA, the Voice of Alaska, with your latest weather report," the newsman announced. "A treacherous arctic storm from Russia is bringing snow to Anchorage and surrounding areas. Continued heavy snowfall is predicted in the mountains, along with sub-zero temperatures. Avalanche danger in those areas is considered extreme. Road equipment within the city limits hasn't been able to keep up, so the authorities are recommending that everyone stay at home. Schools will be closed on Monday and will remain so for the duration of the storm, which is now anticipated to last until the end of the week."

Karen hugged herself after she turned off the TV. She went to the front window and peered out at the falling snow and dark grey sky. The whole neighborhood was blanketed in white, and the houses across the street had their lights on, even though it was midday. The scene looked like a Christmas card, but it was only October. No one anticipated this storm.

Her phone rang. It was Pattie again.

"Sorry to keep calling you, but I'm really worried about the guys. I just watched the weather report and it looks like it's getting worse, not better. Do you think they're okay?"

"I hope so. I know this is scary, but Jim knows how to survive in the bush and he'll do whatever it takes to keep them safe. We have to stay calm and trust his judgment."

"Okay." There was a long pause. "Would you mind if I came over? I'm going crazy here by myself."

"Sure. I think that's a great idea, but please wait until the roads are cleared so it's safe to drive. Bring an overnight bag and we'll wait out this storm together."

***

"Okay, Ronnie, this storm is getting worse. We have to stay ahead of it so here's what we're going to do," Jim said as the two men huddled inside their tent with a lit oil lantern, trying to stay warm. Jim was used to taking charge of situations when things got dicey and still felt confident despite their circumstances. "The lake is freezing fast and we can't let the floats get trapped. We'll need to make a ramp to get the plane out of the water and up onto the beach."

"And how are we going to do that?" Ronnie asked.

"By shoveling a lot and tramping down the snow with our feet."

"Jesus," Ronnie said with a scowl.

"It will work. Once we get the plane out and turned around, I can take off across the lake even if it freezes solid."

"Have you ever done that?"

"No, but I've seen it done on Lake Hood. It'll work. I'm sure of it."

"Okay, but even if we get it out of the water, which is saying a lot, how do we turn it around to face the lake? That's one big heavy airplane."

"I'll tie a rope around one of the wing struts. When I get the plane up on the beach, I'll add power and air rudder while you pull on the rope to turn us around. It'll work, trust me."

Ronnie grimaced in response. "If you say so."

"I say so." Jim got to his feet and offered a gloved hand to help Ronnie up. "Come on, let's get to it. We can't wait any longer."

Ronnie frowned but took the offered hand without protest.

Layered in every piece of clothing they'd brought with them, Jim and Ronnie worked in the howling wind, shoveling snow aside, and stomping and tramping and smoothing it down. Once they had a big enough pad for the plane to slide up and turn around, Jim took the shovel over to the plane and chipped the ice off the floats, while Ronnie kept moving on the beach, giving their smoothed-down area another once over. Satisfied they'd done enough, Jim climbed up and prepared to get inside the plane. He clapped the snow from his gloves, dusted off his clothes, and kicked his boots clean, before opening the pilot-side door and climbing in.

"Ready?" Jim yelled out the window from the cockpit to make his voice heard over the wind.

Ronnie grabbed the rope tied to the wing strut, held it taut, and waved back.

"Okay. When I signal, pull hard. I'm going to start the engine."

Jim turned on the master switch—mixture full rich, a slight shot of the primer, then hit the starter. The prop made a half turn, then stopped dead.

"Shit," Jim cursed under his breath, then yelled out the pilot side window to Ronnie again. "The engine's frozen up."

"Shit, Jim!" Ronnie yelled back. "You got any more brilliant ideas?"

"Cut me some slack, I'm doing my best. And yeah, I do have another brilliant idea."

Jim climbed out, stepped down off the floats onto the packed snow, and made his way back to their tent while Ronnie waited on the beach and stamped his feet to stay warm. A minute later, Jim returned with their Coleman lantern and his sleeping bag. With the lantern fired up again, he opened the oil access door on the engine cowling, slid the lantern inside, closed the door, and wrapped the sleeping bag around the cowling.

"There. We'll give that a few hours to warm up the engine then try again," he told Ronnie, who had come up alongside to see what he was doing. "Let's go stoke up the fire and warm up. We've still got plenty of coffee. A hot cup will do us both good."

Two hours later, Jim laid his hands on the engine compartment. Warmth emanated through his gloves. "Think it's good to go now. Let's get the floats freed from the ice again and give it another try." After chipping the ice off around the floats once more, they removed the sleeping bag and lantern and took up their positions for the same drill. Jim in the cockpit, Ronnie on the ground, rope in hand.

Jim uttered a little prayer as he went through the start-up again—master on, mixture full rich, a shot of prime. Holding his breath, he hit the starter. The big 300-horsepower Continental engine roared to life. He smiled as he let the engine warm up a bit. He added more power and the airplane crept forward then stopped when it touched the snow. Adding more power the plane slid forward continuing to move ahead smoothly gliding up the gentle slope of the packed-down snow. Once completely up on the beach, he hit full power with full rudder and waved Ronnie to pull on the rope.

Ronnie went into action and the airplane spun 180 degrees just as planned. When the nose pointed toward the icy water,

Jim powered down. Seeing the long lake in front of him, he breathed a sigh of relief knowing he could get them out of here now even if it froze solid.

"Woohoo!" yelled Ronnie. He did a little victory dance with arms in the air. "Cowabunga, dude, we did it."

Jim had to laugh at Ronnie's impromptu performance. He jumped down from the plane, walked over, and patted Ronnie's shoulder. "Good job turning us around. Now we just have to wait for this storm to let up. Once visibility clears, we'll get out. Meanwhile, we need to keep the wings and tail clear of snow so the plane's ready for that break in the weather."

"No problemo. We got the hard part done now. It can't snow forever, right?"

Chapter 5
The temp keeps dropping

October 30, 1973

After getting the plane out of the water, Jim and Ronnie spent the rest of the day trying to stay warm. They wore everything they'd brought—long johns under thick wool sweaters, heavy flannel pants, and two pairs of socks inside waterproof Sorel Pac boots. The hoods of their parkas pulled tight around their heads kept the snow from creeping down their necks, and wool scarfs wrapped over their faces warmed the air enough so that they could inhale without icy daggers stabbing their lungs. Where they breathed through the scarves, white crystals hung like tiny stalactites.

The snow kept falling and the temperature kept dropping. As the day went on, it became increasingly difficult to keep the fire going. They had trodden down a path from the tent to the fire pit and the plane, but everywhere else the snow was deepening. When the layer of white grew too thick on the plane, they threw ropes over the wings and dragged the ropes from one end to the other. Most of the dislodged snow fell on their heads in the process. In the bitter cold, they couldn't stay away from the fire for long before numbness in their feet and fingers set in.

"Goddamn, that hurts," Ronnie complained, holding his hands out to the flames again.

"Pain's good," Jim grunted, feeling needles stabbing through his fingers and toes, "means you don't have frostbite."

Seeing the flames flicker and spit in the falling snow, he stabbed the fire with the iron poker and added another log. He thought of Old Red and never felt so thankful to anyone for the simple act of leaving a pile of wood on the ground. This fire would have burned out long ago if all they'd had was the small amount of wood Jim brought. He shook his head and mentally scolded himself for not being better prepared. "Let's cook up the rest of these fish while we still can. Not sure how long we're going to be able to keep this fire going."

When the fish were cooked, they took their hot food and steaming coffee into the tent to eat. It was a relief to get inside where snow wasn't falling continually on their heads. Jim unwrapped the scarf from his face, cracking the stiff fabric so that the ice crystals shattered and fell to the ground. The air in the tent was nearly as cold as outside, but the warm food and coffee soon filled their bellies and brought them some comfort.

After they finished eating and rested awhile, Ronnie looked over at Jim. "You think we should go back out there and clear the snow off the wings again?"

Jim shook his head. "No point. The day's almost over. Might as well stay warm in here and wait till this storm finishes dumping. Let's get into our sleeping bags and try to get some shut-eye. Hopefully, we'll have better luck tomorrow."

Jim woke to an eerie high-pitched moaning, like the warning ululations of a banshee shrieking in the distance. And the sides of the tent were flapping. "Ah, shit." He grabbed his flashlight, unzipped the tent, and looked out. The beam lit a blizzard of blowing snow and their plane twenty feet away—

jumping, twisting, and rocking side to side. "Ronnie! Wake up! We have to tie down the plane or we're going to lose her."

Tying down the plane on the snow-covered beach meant pounding stakes into the frozen ground underneath. Ronnie and Jim had to scream at each other to be heard over the howling wind as they raced to retie the ropes going from the wing loops and struts to newly placed augers. Jim blamed himself again for not being prepared. He'd relied on half-buried logs to hold the plane in place—perfectly sufficient in most cases, drastically short-sighted in this one. He checked Ronnie's knots and pulled hard on the ropes to be sure they were taut. A gust of wind knocked him back, but the plane stayed put. "Okay, that's good!" he yelled and waved for Ronnie to return to the tent. They had to get out of this wind or they were going to freeze. The plane's temp gauge read ten below, and with the wind chill factor, it must be down to minus thirty. It didn't take long to die in that kind of temperature.

***

Tuesday afternoon, October 30, 1973

"Anchorage Flight Service, this is Ted speaking."

"Hi, my name is Karen Wilson. I hate to bother you but my husband and a friend flew out of Lake Hood Friday to go on a fishing trip and planned to be back yesterday. They're probably fine, just waiting for the weather to clear, but—"

"No, you did the right thing," said Ted. "A storm like this can ground the best of them. Can you give me some details—airplane type, tail number, occupants, and destination?

"Yes, or some of it at least. It's a Cessna 185, number N5416R. The pilot is James Wilson and his friend is Ronnie King."

"And where were they going?" asked Ted.

"That's the problem. I'm not exactly sure. They were looking for some special lake they heard about way back in the Talkeetna Mountains. I don't know if they even filed a flight plan."

"I see," replied Ted. "Can you tell me the color of the plane?"

"Purple and white.

"And they took off from Lake Hood? On floats?"

"Yes."

"Okay, I think I have enough information now."

"Jim's a really good pilot. He owns an air taxi and maintenance operation on Lake Hood and has been flying the backcountry for many years.

"Good to know. I'll issue an advisory to keep an eye out for them. We can't get any planes in the air to go looking until this storm clears, but since he's as experienced as you said, they're probably fine. Please let us know if you hear from them."

"I will. Thank you so much!"

***

"Do you... do you think the girls are freaking out?" asked Ronnie. He sat upright inside his sleeping bag but still shivered. The tent walls continued to ripple, and the wind outside still moaned.

Jim sighed. "Probably. We missed our return deadline twenty-four hours ago." He looked over at their pile of frozen fish. "At least, we won't starve, assuming we can get a fire going again."

Ronnie grunted in disgust, "If I never eat another grayling again in my whole life that would be fine with me."

"Yeah, I'm sick of fish too." Maybe it's time to get out the rations. I didn't want to unless we absolutely had to, but ...

"I thought you said there's enough to last us a week. You don't think we're going to be stuck here that long, do you?"

Jim shrugged. "No, I—I just like to be cautious. We should get a break in this weather soon."

"Hope you're right. Seems like it's just getting colder and colder. And that lake looks like it's completely frozen over now. Good thing we got the airplane out in time."

"Yeah, a good thing." Jim noticed Ronnie's teeth chattering, not a good sign. Jim had plenty of meat on him for insulation. Poor skinny surfer dude, Ronnie, wasn't used to this kind of weather. He thought for a moment and came to a decision. "I need to be doing something. You know how I hate sitting around. Think I'll go out and check the plane again and bring back our survival gear."

Ronnie started to push his way out of his sleeping bag, clearly intending to join him, until Jim held up a hand. "Nah, you just stay here, keep warm. I don't need help. If I get cold, I'll just crawl inside the plane to get out of the wind and warm up again, before I come back, so don't worry if I'm gone for a bit."

Ronnie scowled at him, but when Jim smiled confidently and patted him on the knee, he nodded and pulled the sleeping bag up over his shoulders again. "Fine!"

Jim slipped out of the tent as quickly as he could and reclosed it. Turning around to make his way to the plane, he was confronted by a complete white-out with no division between the ground and the sky. Just blowing snow and white upon white, everywhere. He could only see a few feet ahead but followed the path they'd made, passing by the snow-covered fire pit on his way to the plane. He found it still tied down tight, the ropes straining to keep it there. Best he could do. Now what he needed to do was make sure Ronnie didn't freeze to death.

He stepped up on the floats and got their shovel and survival gear out of the baggage compartment then worked his way back through the wind on the path to their tent. There he started shoveling, building a wall of snow around the tent to block the wind and seal in whatever heat they could generate inside. He was building an igloo of sorts. He had to be careful not to sweat too much in the process. Every bit of moisture he generated would quickly turn to ice.

Chapter 6
The flight out

Thursday, November 1, 1973

Two more days had passed—two days of huddling inside their tent protected by a wall of snow, eating cold rations, with nothing but lit candles and their body heat to keep them warm—getting to know each other way more intimately than either of them ever wanted to, getting on each other's nerves in the process. Turned out Ronnie liked to chew his fingernails down to the quick which made Jim grimace in disgust. And Ronnie complained Jim's nose whistled when he slept.

Jim woke to Ronnie jostling him. "Dammit, put some cotton in your ears if it bothers you so much."

"Come on, dude, wake up! I think it's finally clearing! I can see sunlight coming through the clouds. The wind's stopped blowing and the snow's let up."

The anger vanished. "Okay, I'm up. I'm up!"

The last time Jim had ventured out, he'd seen nothing but white, and the wind had howled in his ears. Now all lay quiet in a snow-covered world that sparkled in the light. He shaded his eyes and looked up at the sky. The thick grey clouds hadn't left but the ceiling looked at least a hundred feet up and a golden glow seeped through. Most importantly, he could see the walls of the canyon.

"This looks like the break we've been waiting for. We better get moving! There's no telling how long it'll last. I'll get the

Coleman lantern and start warming the engine while you load up our gear, and then I'll help you get the wings and tail cleared. Don't bother with the tent. Just leave it where it is."

They both went to work. By the time the plane was loaded and cleared of snow, the engine cowling felt warm.

Jim looked up at the sky again, still clouded over, but the canyon itself lay open which meant he should be able to find the exit and work his way out. "Should" is the cautionary word. There was no telling what they would fly into. It wasn't a decision he wanted to make alone.

"What do you think, Ronnie? Should we try it?"

"I'm all for getting out of here, but you're the captain. It's your call."

Jim nodded, feeling the full weight of responsibility back on his shoulders. He stared at the sky, debating with himself. He looked at Ronnie shivering again and knew he needed to get this California kid out of here. "Okay, let's give it a go. Hopefully, once we're out of the canyon these clouds will lift."

They climbed into the plane and strapped in. Jim fired up the big engine, letting it idle to bring up the oil temp and warm the cabin. He added power did a quick control and instrument check cycled the prop and lowered the flaps to 20 degrees. He pulled the cockpit heat control to full heat and switched on the pitot heat. "Ready?"

"Ready, Big Kahuna." Ronnie spread his thumb and little finger apart and wriggled his hand at him.

Jim added more power, but the airplane didn't move. *The floats must be frozen to the ground.* He went to full power and started rocking the airplane with the elevators. Finally, the floats broke loose, and the plane accelerated down from their handmade ramp and out across the frozen lake. The floats plowed through the wind-driven snowdrifts and screeched against the ice as Jim gently worked the elevator control to keep them level. He heard the keels scrape until the plane reached flying speed and lifted into the air.

Jim quickly glanced at the instrument panel and realized his flight instruments were frozen. No airspeed, altitude, heading, attitude, or vertical speed.......Shit! Oh well, he knew his airplane well enough he could fly by feel. The instruments would eventually warm up and come to life.

"Yeah!" Ronnie crowed. "We're out of here!"

Jim said nothing, knowing they were far from *out*. He banked the plane gently and aimed toward the canyon exit, unable to climb more than a hundred feet due to the thick low clouds above them that would deny all visibility. He pulled back the power and leveled off, leaving the flaps at 20 degrees for slow flight. The windshield started fogging up from their warm breath so Jim diverted the cabin heat to the full windshield defroster position which still only gave him about a twelve-inch circle to see outside.

At the end of the canyon, the grey ceiling lifted enough that he was able to climb another hundred feet. With each foot gained, his confidence rose with it. Maybe this foray would prove successful and they wouldn't have to turn back. The trouble was, flying this low with cliffs on all sides meant he had no frame of reference. He was lost.

"Wish I'd paid better attention to all the twists and turns we made coming in here. I figured we'd just climb up over the mountains and fly directly back to Anchorage, but now we're stuck down here inside the canyons. Help me out, Ronnie. Look at the chart again and find me the way out of here."

"Okay." Ronnie fumbled with the chart, squinting at it. "I think I kind of remember the way. Try turning into that next canyon up there." He pointed to a craggy opening coming up on their right. "Pretty sure that's how we came in here."

As Jim angled for the opening, a rocky spire jumped out of the mist ahead. "You sure? I don't remember that rock formation."

"No, I'm not sure. I'm guessing just like you. But we can always turn around if it's not right. Right?"

"Right," Jim said but knew it wouldn't be that simple. There was little room to maneuver with these canyon walls on all sides. "I'll keep the airspeed as slow as I can." He noted he still had no airspeed or altimeter indications from his instruments.

Heading in with a dogleg turn, they flew into a thick fog bank and visibility dropped to zero. Jim applied full power and quickly rolled into a steep turn, flying blind with no instruments he tried desperately not to stall and spin. The airplane shuttered and the stall warning horn blared as they made the turn.

"Holy shit!" Ronnie grabbed hold of the strap next to him.

Jim rolled out of the turn and lowered the nose as he pulled the power back.

"Zero visibility that way!"

"Think I just wet my pants!"

Jim was straining to see out the still partially obscured windshield when he saw what he'd been hoping for. "Hey, look. Up ahead. I see daylight above that ridge. Looks like we got a hole in the weather. If I can get us up through there, we are out of here."

Starting the best angle of climb Jim added full power, prop full climb pitch, flaps 20 degrees, and guessing at the airspeed, he flew upward, climbing with the terrain, aiming toward the beckoning blue in the sky above the hill.

Just before reaching the crest, the blue disappeared, and the ceiling layer went all the way to the ground, socked in. A complete whiteout. Only now did he realize the small circle of blue had been what pilots call a sucker hole. Looking up from beneath it, he'd been fooled into thinking he'd found an escape hole through the clouds. Now he was flying blind, low and slow, with no choice but to turn back. He rolled hard to the left into a sixty-degree bank, trying to escape the cloud that now engulfed them like a shroud. Both Ron and the stall warning horn were screaming at him, but all his concentration was focused on coaxing the airplane around, praying they were still high enough to clear the rising cliffs

Flying blind in a white-out with the flight instruments still frozen, Jim could only go by feel. After completing what he thought was a 180-degree turn they were dangerously close to stalling. Jim had to lower the nose to gain airspeed. As the mist thinned he saw dark rocks jutting up that looked only feet below. Without realizing it, he instinctively pulled back on the controls to lift the nose. The crest of the mountain ahead to their right promised escape if he could reach it.

Jim willed the plane upward as he gently milked the controls on the ragged edge of a stall. "Come on, come on, only a couple hundred feet to go."

The stall warning horn blared, and the airplane buffeted, the controls turning to mush. They were pitched too high, flying too slow, and on the verge of falling from the sky.

"We're not going to make it!" Ronnie yelled.

With a sharp curse, Jim shoved the nose forward kicked the left rudder, and yanked the control yoke into a steep left turn. The airplane responded coming around ninety degrees, flying them down the face of the mountain. The floats hit and plowed through layers of newly fallen snow and ice beneath.

Caught now in the grip of the mountain, the plane shot down the slope unable to free itself even though they were picking up speed at an alarming rate. Jim struggled to keep the plane from skidding sideways and going into a spin. Chunks of ice and snow flew over the nose of the plane as if they were following a snow blower down a ski jump. Jim tried to steer with the rudder and see through the ice flying into the windscreen.

I have to get us back in the air.

"Hang on!" Jim shouted and pulled back hard on the control yoke and the flap handle. With full power and full flaps, the nose lifted and for a split second, he enjoyed the crazy notion they would fly off again, then a large outcropping of rocks appeared in front of him. He swerved to the left and the right wing hit the rocks, sending them into a spin down the sixty-degree slope, and careening the two men inside like dice in a rolling can. He heard Ronnie screaming, and then something hit Jim hard on the head and everything went black.

Chapter 7
The crash

November 1, 1973

"Okay guys, listen up," Air Force Colonel Bardon commanded his search and rescue team. "We have a missing Cessna 185 lost somewhere back in the Talkeetna mountains, seven days overdue. Two men aboard. Could be they're just holding up till the weather clears, but we're going to go take a look and keep our ears on for a beacon in case they have a problem. The weather's still too nasty for Civil Air Patrol so it's just us for now, and we won't have long to search. It's supposed to close back in around 1300 hours. Understood?" He waited for heads to nod, then circled his arm in the air. "Let's roll."

***

"Jim, Jim. Come on, buddy, wake up. Jim. Jim!"

The annoying voice and rough hands shaking his shoulder gradually pierced through the pain and the fog. Jim opened his eyes and squinted at Ronnie's face until it came into focus. "What? What happened?"

"We crashed, man! I smell fuel. We need to get out." Ronnie's eyes were wide in alarm.

Jim pressed a hand to the rising welt on his forehead as memory flooded back. He tried to take stock of the situation. The plane was sharply pitched, its nose pointing down the mountain—*bad*, but it was upright, which meant he wasn't hanging from his seat belt—*good*. He smelled fuel, too—*bad*; but no hint of fire—*good*. Jim released his belt and twisted to look around. "Ow!" Sharp pain in his side made him gasp—*uh oh*. He lifted his shirt to take a look—the skin was intact, but he had no doubt that the ribs beneath were cracked or at least badly bruised. He took a deeper breath, fearing the result, but felt no worse for it. He nodded and smiled in relief. *No lung punctured. Best news yet.*

"We're alive and seem to be in pretty good shape, all things considered."

"Speak for yourself." Ronnie gestured at his right leg.

Jim could only see as far down as Ronnie's knee. The lower half lay hidden beneath the crushed instrument panel "Oh shit. How bad?"

"I don't know, but it hurts like hell and my leg's trapped. Help me get out of here before this thing goes up in flames with me in it. That would piss me off."

"That's not going to happen," Jim said with more conviction than maybe he had a reason for. He reached between the seats and pulled the shovel out of the back then positioned it beside Ronnie's trapped leg.

"So, you're okay?" Ronnie asked.

"Yeah, I think so, 'except for a screaming headache and painful ribs. Lucky for us, the snow cushioned our fall."

"You've got that right, and that's one hell of a drop-off just beyond where we crashed." Ronnie shook his head.

Between the headache, dizziness, and shortness of breath from his aching ribs and the awkwardness of using a shovel for leverage, it took a lot of strength to force the metal back. As he leaned hard on the shovel, the panel groaned in protest but gave way. "Try it now."

Ronnie pulled at his knee with both hands, grimacing in pain. With a sharp cry, his foot came free, revealing the damage. Blood seeped through his pant leg just above his boot.

"Can you get out on your side? "Jim yelled.

Ronnie released his belt and unlatched the door. It fell open under the force of gravity. "Oh shit! No way, man. I got nothing' but the air over here."

"Okay, its okay, just slide over towards me. I'll get you out on my side."

"Yeah, okay." Ronnie started scooting over as Jim pushed open his door, threw the shovel outside, and crawled free. "We better hurry. I'm worried about that fuel running down the cowling. It could light off on the exhaust manifold."

"I know, I know!" Jim pulled Ronnie out, even as a sharp pain shot through his side. Once freed from the cockpit, he helped Ronnie hop on his good left leg over to a boulder that was bare of snow.

"Wait here while I get our survival gear and the emergency beacon!" Jim turned back to the airplane just as the fuel ignited in a *whoosh.* Flames raced over the front of the plane and up across the wings containing the fuel tanks.

"Stay down!" Jim yelled, "I've got to get the locator beacon out of the tail section before it burns up or they'll never find us."

Jim lifted his head to look over the boulder. The front half of the plane was on fire, but the back was as yet untouched, which meant there was still hope.

Jim saw now that fire dripped from the wings onto the floats beneath, where the extra fuel canisters were stored.

Jim braced himself for a mad dash.

Ronnie grabbed hold of his parka and hung on. "Forget it, man. It's too dangerous."

"Dammit!" Jim crouched back down, knowing Ronnie was right. The explosion was deafening, the sound echoed off the rocky cliffs above. Seconds later, there was another explosion, and then another—both fuel cans going up one after the other. There was nothing left to explode now so Jim got to his feet to check the damage. What was left of the cockpit and tail section was fully engulfed in flames. All he could do was watch his plane and supplies burn.

Ronnie pushed against the boulder to stand on his good leg. "Sorry about your plane, man."

Jim shrugged. "Never liked the color anyway." He held out his hands to the fire. "Enjoy the warmth while it lasts, because we're going to be getting real cold real soon. All our survival gear is still inside that burning mess. I don't think we'll be able to salvage any of it."

As the flames burned, the snow melted into rivulets and the wreckage sank lower. A large crack ran crookedly across the face of the slope high above the plane. Seeing it grow, Jim took a step back. There was a muffled rumbling, then growing louder……

"Avalanche!" Jim spun toward Ronnie and tackled him, taking him down behind the boulders again just as the mountain let go of its load. Deep layers of snow, and ice beneath cracked and slid away, a huge wave of white barreling down the mountainside like a roaring freight train, enveloping their flaming airplane wreckage and carrying it away. The boulders protected Jim and Ronnie from getting caught up in the wave, but flying snow and ice crystals layered them in white. When the rumbling stopped, and all sound lay muted, Jim raised his snow-covered head. "You okay?"

Ronnie looked back at him, his face decorated with white crystals. "I think so. You?"

Jim nodded and helped Ronnie up. They knocked the snow off their clothing and faces,

"You're not going to tackle me again are you?" Ronnie asked, wearing a grin.

"No guarantees."

They wrapped their scarves over their mouths and pulled their parka hoods up. As Ronnie looked around at the forbidding white world surrounding them, his face lost any sign of humor as he registered the seriousness of their situation. Jim had no words of comfort to offer. He saw the same thing. No trees, no shelter of any kind, just lichen-covered rocks bordering the sides of a steep snowy crevasse with their plane nowhere to be seen.

"Well, this is just freaking great. What do we do now?" Ronnie asked.

"Rule one is never leaving the plane, so we go down after it. Even burned out, it's shelter, and a lot more visible to search planes than we are. Doubt the beacon's working anymore, though."

"You think?"

The familiar drone of an aircraft came in the distance, and both men looked up.

"Seriously? Now they show up?" Ronnie waved his hands in the air.

"You know they can't see us, right?"

"I know that. It's just what you do. You wave. Give me a break." Ronnie whipped off his watch cap and threw it down on the snow in a fit of frustration.

"Well, the good news is our emergency locator would have been transmitting, at least it should have been until it burned up," Jim said.

"You think they heard it?"

"Possibly." Jim stared up at the grey sky.

"Does that mean they know where we are?"

"Possibly." He knew from doing search and rescue missions himself, that if the missing party was spotted, the plane would circle directly above to let them know. Instead, the drone of the engine was fading into the distance. "This cloud cover's just too thick."

"But they'll be back, right?" Ronnie asked.

"Sure," Jim said, although it was anyone's guess. He had no idea if that plane was truly searching for them, and even if it was, whether it heard their beacon, let alone determined from where it originated. Odds were against every one of those possibilities.

***

"Mrs. Walker, this is Ted at Flight Service, I called to give you a quick update. A search plane out of Elmendorf picked up an ELT signal this morning, then lost it. They flew around the area for several hours but never picked it up again. Unfortunately, they couldn't establish ground visibility due to heavy cloud coverage. Civil Air Patrol is also on alert and they'll start searching as soon as we get visual flight conditions. I'm sorry. I wish I could tell you more."

"I'm sure you're doing everything you can, thanks for keeping me updated," said Karen. When she hung up the phone, she relayed the information to Pattie, who'd been camped out at her home since this all began. When Pattie broke into tears, Karen hugged her hard. "They'll make it back, I know they will. Jim knows how to handle himself in the wilderness more than almost anyone and would never let anyone get hurt on his watch. Don't you worry. He'll get them home." As she held onto her young friend, a plan started to form in her mind. She believed in Jim's survival skills, but just sitting around waiting for someone else to take charge wasn't her nature.

"Pattie, you and I need to go find Old Red."

Chapter 8
Climbing down the mountain

November 1, 1973

Jim stood on the tallest of the boulders to peer down the slope trying to see some sign of his airplane below. All he saw was broken ice and snow, and a jagged landscape of bluish-white rocky cliffs bordered the slope on both sides with jutting rocks above and below them. Every direction looked equally forbidding. He knew they needed to get down this mountain, but there was no easy path, and Ronnie's injury would make it doubly hard.

"Maybe we should just wait here for search and rescue to find us," Ronnie suggested. He sat on a smaller rock with his leg stretched out in front of him, supported by their one remaining tool—the shovel Jim had thrown out of the plane.

"They'll never spot us down here without a signal fire." Jim looked around at the barren rocks, scowling. He jumped down from the boulder grimacing and sucking in a ragged breath as pain shot through his ribs. He kicked the snow away from the rock edges hoping to find buried tufts of weedy tundra, which would burn. Nope, nothing but lichen. He sat down gently next to Ronnie. "Shit."

"Yeah…Shit." Ronnie sighed then took a big inhalation. "You should go. You can make it out on your own."

Jim glared at him. "Don't go there, I'm not leaving you. We'll figure this out. Let's start by taking inventory." He patted his chest feeling the reassuring lumps underneath. "I have my pistol, fully loaded, and extra ammo, my hunting knife, compass, and some beef jerky. What have you got?"

"Hell, if I know. Pattie messed with my parka, stuffing all the pockets, but I never really looked." He started feeling around and pulling out baggies. "Okay, let's see...here's a couple of Snickers, some more jerky, glove liners, and instant hand warmers. Oh, look, a Swiss Army knife. That'll come in handy when I decide to slit my throat."

"Freezing to death is better," Jim replied.

"Good to know." Ronnie's eyebrows rose as he pulled a large freezer-sized plastic bag from his inside pocket. It was stuffed to the brim with a typed list of items taped to its exterior. "Huh, what the heck is all this?" He read the list aloud...

"The Poor Man's Survival Kit:
- **"One 55-gallon trash bag for rain shelter, sleeping bag, chemical protection, floatation device, water still, container, sling, etc.**
- **One N95 dust/mist respirator for protection from chemical, biological, and radiological hazards**

He snickered. "Guess that's in case someone drops a nuke on us...

- **One single-edge S/S razor blade**...

"S/S?"

"Stainless steel."

"Oh, right." He read on...

"...for last resort defense, cutting tool, escape."

Ronnie laughed. "Defense, seriously?"

"What else?"

"Okay. Um…

- **One 12 by 24-inch sheet of aluminum foil. For signaling reflector, heat reflector, cooking pot, water collection, boiling, and wound covering.**
- **One 12-inch by 24-foot sheet of plastic wrap. For eye protection, container, wound covering, and splint holding.**
- **Ten twelve-foot lengths of electrical tape wound on cardboard. For repair of clothing and shelter, wound protection, and general repairs.**
- **Ten waterproof matches, a striker, and a candle. For fire starting, heat, light, and signals.**
- **One ten-foot length of 25-pound nylon fishing line. For fishing, shelter building, trapping, and repairs.**
- **Four safety pins. For repairs, fishing, securing clothing, and slings.**
- **One coffee filter. For water filtration, and fire starting.**
- **Four sugar packets. For energy.**
- **Four aspirin. For pain relief, and heart attack reduction.**"

Ronnie stopped reading and handed the bag to Jim. "Guess all that stuff's inside there. Pattie's a stickler for being prepared. Ex-Girl Scout and daughter of a retired Marine and all."

"I'll be damned." Jim smiled behind his ice-encrusted scarf. "Your wife may have just saved our lives."

"With that Girl Scout stuff?"

"Hokey, I agree, but we just went from near zero assets to quite a few." Jim pulled the plastic wrap out of the bag. "I can use this to secure that shovel to your leg for a splint. If you can walk on it, we can get down off this mountain." He worked as he talked, first unwrapping then re-wrapping the plastic around Ronnie's leg and the shovel, handle end up, shovel end down. He secured it all with a length of electrical tape. "There, that should give you some support. Try standing on it."

Ronnie pushed off the rock and gingerly put weight on the braced leg. He grimaced but took a lurching step. "Ugh! Shit! Still hurts like hell."

"Sorry. Think you can manage?"

Ronnie nodded and took another step. "Yeah. I'll make it."

"I'll go slowly and try to step where I step."

"Okay, Kahuna, lead the way and try not to take us over a cliff. One crash today was enough."

Jim edged his way down through the deep snow. Sometimes it buried him up to his chest. Flailing and sliding, straining and panting he struggled to clear a path for Ronnie. Occasionally, searing pain in his ribs brought him up short, but after a moment he went on and made sure Ronnie followed. After about 50 yards, they rested, then started down again. They couldn't afford to get too overheated in these subzero temperatures where sweat-soaked clothes could turn ice hard. Over and over they scooted downward, taking breaks and bracing against rocky outcroppings before moving on again. Suddenly they came upon a sharp vertical drop-off and started to slide.

Jim threw himself backward into Ronnie and dug in his feet trying to stop their forward momentum. They nearly slid into free flight before Ronnie's shovel-edged foot jammed into the ice and saved them both. Poised with his feet hanging over the cliff's edge, Jim looked down into the crevasse that nearly claimed them. A sheep could jump it, or run up the cliff face, but there was no way for a man to cross. More exposed boulders lay to their left. Nearly breathless, he waved in that direction. "Scoot over to those rocks."

They crawled sideways and pulled themselves to safety.

"We'll have to backtrack and try to find another way down."

Panting, Ronnie nodded, too spent to reply. They sat on the exposed rock and leaned against the cliff at their backs. Ronnie closed his eyes to rest, but Jim kept looking around, exploring the area with his eyes, searching for a way out. And then finally he saw it, a narrow line, a ribbon of tan against deep brown, running downward across the face of a cliff in the distance. He leaned forward and squinted, hoping to God that he wasn't imagining it. If he was seeing right, he'd spotted an animal trail. Protected by a rock wall, it appeared to be out of the wind, and free of snow. He shook Ronnie and pointed. "Look. Over there. Can you see it? That line going across? I think it's a sheep trail."

The Big Horn sheep lived in these mountains taking refuge from predators along the steep rocks but they make frequent forays below in search of grasses and mineral licks.

The more he stared at that wriggly sloping line in the distance, the more certain he was that it promised a way down from this mountain.

"We need to get over to that trail."

Ronnie sheltered his eyes with a gloved hand and peered at the line sketched across the face of the cliff in the distance. "How far away do you think it is?"

"Hard to judge. Could be half a mile, could be a lot more." He glanced at the watch on his wrist. We've got about four hours of daylight left. We need to get moving."

After three hours of slogging through deep snow and scrambling over exposed rocks, the line in the distance appeared little if any closer. They took a long break on some more outcroppings to share Jim's beef jerky, and snow-water melted in a bowl made of aluminum foil from Pattie's "Survival Kit". The sunlight glinted through the water, reflecting off the foil to light up their faces as they drank.

"It's further than I thought," Jim admitted. "We'll probably have to spend the night up here."

Ronnie's eyes widened. "Doesn't it get like twenty below?"

Jim nodded. "Yeah, it's gonna get cold. Real cold. We should give ourselves an hour of light to set up camp." He got to his feet. "Here, I'll show you a trick on how to estimate how much time's left until sunset." He helped Ronnie up. "Okay, good, now face the sun and extend your arm. Bend your wrist so your fingers stack up parallel to the horizon." He demonstrated and watched Ronnie mimic him. "Position it so it looks like the sun's sitting on your top finger. Got it?"

Ronnie nodded.

"Each finger between the sun and the horizon, or in this case the edge of the mountain, equals about 15 minutes, so when it gets down to four fingers, you've got about an hour before sunset." He squinted measuring the distance between the bottom of his hand and the mountains in the distance. "I'm guessing we got about two hours of light left. We'll go for another hour, then we need to stop, build a shelter, and wait it out till morning."

Ronnie waved his arm to take in the barren snow-covered landscape. "With what? There's nothing here."

"Packed snow makes good walls. We'll be fine. Come on, let's see how far we can get."

When the sun dipped behind the mountain, the beckoning trail in the distance disappeared in shadow. Jim felt the air temperature dropping and started looking for a good spot to make camp before dark. When they reached a large area of exposed rocks, he came to a halt.

"I need to borrow that shovel," he announced. "Sit down over there and I'll take it off."

"Fine." Ronnie dropped onto a rock and stuck his shovel-supported leg out.

Jim carefully unwrapped the injured leg, saving the plastic wrap and electrical tape for reuse. Once he freed the shovel, he handed the wrappings to Ronnie for safekeeping and went to work, digging a pit in the snow between some large boulders, piling the removed snow up and around to create a small circular structure with a raised floor, a gutter to drain off the melt inside, an entry 90 degrees to the wind and a vent hole in the roof. He made it two man-wide, and half a man tall, just enough room to get inside, stretch out flat, and sit up. He laid the trash bag from Pattie's survival kit on the raised bottom, then crawled back outside. "Okay, you can go in now."

Ronnie shook his head but scooted inside. Jim squeezed in next to him and scooped in a pile of snow to close the small entry door. From a seated position, he wiped down the curved ceiling and walls of their snowy dug-out with his gloved hands to ensure any moisture building up would run down the sides and into the gutter, instead of dripping on their heads. It was difficult to see each other's faces now even though they were only inches apart.

"Well, isn't this cozy," Ronnie said, through chattering teeth. "Not exactly what I'd call warm though."

"Hang in there. That'll change." He placed a small candle on the trash bag floor at their feet and lit a match by raking it with the edge of his thumbnail. The match flashed to life and replaced the dark with dancing shadows. "Get that foil bowl out again. We'll need to melt more snow to drink." As he lit the candle, he noticed how hard Ronnie's hands were shaking as he placed the foil on the floor and scooped snow into it. Despite wearing the same number of layered clothes, Ronnie wasn't handling the cold nearly as well as Jim, whose large stocky build was thoroughly acclimated to this climate. Ronnie's thin California-born body shivered in spasm

As their small shelter gradually captured their body heat and warmth from the candle's flame, Jim could feel the tension in his chilled limbs relax and Ronnie's teeth no longer chattered. They waited for the clump of snow to melt in the foil, watching the painfully slow process with a morbid fascination. By the time the bowl was filled with water, Ronnie had ceased shivering and Jim unzipped his Parka.

Together they shared another meager meal of beef jerky and melted snow water, then split one of the Snicker's bars Pattie had slipped into Ronnie's coat pocket. The warmth and food made Jim's eyelids want to close and he felt his head droop and bob awake again a couple of times. He decided it was warm enough now that he could safely extinguish the half-burned candle. He hoped they wouldn't need it for another night but wanted to play it safe.

"Feeling better?" he asked.

"Yeah sure," Ronnie replied but his voice cracked.

Before snuffing out the candle, Jim lifted it to illuminate his friend's face and was startled to see tears. "Are you in pain? Maybe you should take those aspirins."

Ronnie swiped at his cheeks and eyes, pushing strands of his blond hair away in the process. "Nah, man, I'm okay. Really. I was just thinking about Pattie." He sniffled. "I mean, what if I never see her again?"

"You'll see her. I'm going to get you down off this mountain and you'll see her." Jim spoke with more force than he intended. "No more talk like that. I'm putting out this candle now, and we're going to get some sleep and start fresh in the morning. Got it?"

"Yeah, I got it."

Jim pinched out the flame. In the pitch black, he felt for his pocket and slipped the candle inside, zipped up his jacket, then laid down with his back to Ronnie. A moment later, he felt Ronnie's back pressed against his, and before long came the sound of soft snoring. He needed to do the same, but for some reason, he felt angry as hell and couldn't relax despite the physical exhaustion of his body.

Why am I so pissed off? Ronnie didn't do anything wrong. Just got scared for a minute that he wouldn't see his wife again.

Only then did he realize he hadn't given any thought to his own family. Looking up he saw stars through the narrow opening and wondered if they might be looking at the same sight.

It doesn't matter, he decided. *They're safe at home and don't need me worrying about them. I got enough to deal with just keeping us alive.*

Decision made, he put his wife and son from his mind and fell asleep.

Chapter 9
Finding Old Red

November 1, 1973

"I hate waiting around like this. We need to talk to this Old Red guy. He's the only one who knows exactly where they went," Karen told Pattie. "Maybe we can even get him to take us out there."

"Okay, so, where do we find him—do you even know what he looks like?" Pattie asked.

"No, but I have an idea where to look. Jim likes to hang out at the Super Cub Pub at Lake Hood and swap stories with his flying buddies. This guy might be there right now."

"Then let's go. I'll drive," said Pattie. "Grab your coat."

"Let me get Jamie, he needs to come with us."

It was just past six thirty in the evening and already growing dark when they left the house in Pattie's red four-wheel drive Chevy Blazer.

They drove in silence through the falling snow, the car's heater on full to combat the bitter cold radiating through the windows. A blanket of white covered the road and hillsides creating a surreal wintery scene. The only sounds were that of the engine, the blasting heater, the tires crunching through the snow, and the whap, whap, whap of the windshield wipers.

The parking lot at the Super Cub Pub was full so Pattie parked in front of a dumpster with a sign that read, NO PARKING. "I'm sure no one will care," she said.

"Sorry Jamie you have to wait here, "It's a bar and you're too young to go inside. We'll leave the engine running so you'll be warm enough. Won't be gone long."

The pub was packed and filled with smoke. There didn't seem to be an open seat anywhere.

"Looks like all the grounded pilots decided to hang out here," Karen said.

The loud talk and laughter quieted some as men's heads swiveled toward the two women standing near the entrance. Karen looked back at their faces, not recognizing anyone. She was about to yell out for Old Red when a waitress walked up to rescue them.

"Hi there, ladies. Can I help you?"

"Yes, we're looking for someone. My husband, James Walker, met with him here a couple of weeks ago."

"Oh, you must be Karen. I'm Shirl. Jim's mentioned you."

Pattie stepped forward. "Hi there, I'm Pattie. The reason we're here is our husbands flew out fishing Friday and were supposed to be home by now. We're getting real worried and think this guy we're looking for might be able to help."

"Oh, I'm so sorry. I'm sure they're just fine."

"Thanks, but as we said, they're overdue. A pilot drew them a map to some secret lake of his and we thought maybe we could talk to him. His name's Old Red. Do you know him?"

"That old fart? Oh yeah. I know him. He hangs out here and drinks way too much.

"Is he here?"

"No, sorry, haven't seen him in a few days, but he also likes to hang out at the Birdhouse. He could be there. Do you know the place?"

Karen sighed. "Yes, I know it." She turned to Pattie, "It's down at Bird Creek, almost to Girdwood, a long drive, and in this weather—"

"Hey," Shirl interrupted, "why don't I give them a call and see if he's even there? No point in driving out there if it's for nothing, right?"

"Thank you. We'd appreciate it," Pattie said.

"Be right back." Shirl left then returned a couple minutes later. "Yeah, he's there alright, but he's been drinking awhile."

"We can deal with that," Pattie replied.

"Let's go get him."

"Okay, let's do it." Karen followed Pattie then almost as an afterthought glanced back over her shoulder at Shirl. "Thanks."

"Good luck. Hope it all works out," Shirl yelled as they went out the door.

As they turned onto Seward Highway for the winding twenty-mile drive to Bird Creek, Jamie sat up and looked out the window. "Wait. This isn't the way back."

"No, we have to go to the Birdhouse."

Jamie leaned forward. "No way. The Birdhouse? Really? You have to let me go inside."

Karen frowned and shook her head. "You're a minor."

"Come on, Mom, please. I just want to see it. It's not like I'm going to order a beer or anything. Please, Mom."

"We'll see."

The highway ran between steep mountain cliffs on one side and the bay on the other. The snow was coming down fast. The road was almost deserted for good reason. These cliffs were prone to avalanches and driving this highway could be hazardous at any time but even more so at night and in heavy snow. Pattie drove slowly not letting the car's speed overtake what lay visible in the headlights. The usual thirty-minute drive turned into a nerve-wracking sixty before they reached Bird Creek.

The Birdhouse Bar was an old log cabin that had been converted into a saloon. Above the front entrance hung a six-foot tall garish blue and orange pelican that looked like something a seven-year-old made in school. The entire building leaned at a ten-degree angle and looked ready to fall over if given a hard shove. Cars filled the entire parking area, and nearly all of them were covered with snow indicating they had been there a while.

From personal experience, Karen knew what to expect, but for anyone who hadn't been here before, the place was a shocker. As they stepped inside Pattie and Jamie both froze and stared in amazement. Karen knew they weren't surprised that the place was packed with people, smoke-filled, and loud with laughter and raunchy music from a jukebox, all typical of most bars. What they and no one ever expected was the choice of décor. Not one inch of wall or ceiling space was left uncovered. Colorful women's panties and bras, men's tighty-whities and printed boxer shorts, discarded ties, scarfs and T-shirts, miscellaneous notes, letters, napkins, photographs, business cards, greeting cards, and whatever else it occurred to the patrons in the middle of a drunken moment of inspiration to be a necessary addition had found a home on the walls and ceilings of the Bird House Bar.

The place was packed and from the sound of it, everyone seemed to be rip-roaring drunk and having a great time. All the tables, chairs, and bar stools—sawed-off tree stumps nailed to the floor—were filled along with most of the floor space. It was standing room only.

"Wait till I tell the guys," Jamie exclaimed

Karen looked at Jamie staring around with his mouth open. "Okay, you saw it, now go wait in the car."

"What? Seriously? But—okay"

Karen went back to where Pattie was waiting. Together, they elbowed through the crowd over to the bar and waved for the attention of the lady bartender who was nearly as wide as the bar she tended. Karen had to shout to be heard, "Is there a guy named Old Red here?"

"Honey," the woman yelled back, "he's been here for the last two days. You must be the gals, Shirl called about. That's him over at the corner table, the one in the hat." She pointed a beefy arm toward the back of the room. "If you can get him out of here, drinks are on the house."

Karen turned to look. What she glimpsed through the crowd didn't give her much hope. The one in the hat had to be one of the oldest, scruffiest-looking men she'd ever seen, with long hair and a straggly beard, both filthy and unkempt, just like his clothing.

"I got this," Pattie said and shoved ahead through the crowd. Karen stayed close behind listening to Pattie declining invitations for a drink, a dance, and a few unmentionable offers before reaching Old Red's table.

He was slumped over his beer, his head held up in his hand with one elbow propped on the table, and his other arm in free flight to illustrate something he was telling two young men seated across from him. He stopped in mid-sentence seeing the two women standing next to him. "Well, well, hello there, ladies. How about letting me buy you a beer?" Old Red winked at them. He glared at the two men across from him and waved his arms for them to get up. "You fellers get up out of there. Let these nice ladies sit down and go get them a beer."

Startled into action, the two young men jumped up to make room. Pattie and Karen quickly took the empty bench when they had the chance.

"No thanks, we're not here to drink," said Karen raising her voice to be heard over the roar of the packed room. Old Red's grin aimed at Pattie turned into squinted displeasure as he looked at Karen. "I'm Jim Walker's wife, and this is Pattie, Ronnie's wife. Our guys flew out to some secret lake of yours last Friday and haven't come back."

Old Red guffawed and waved a hand at them. "It's just this weather. They're holdin' up till it clears, just like the rest of us."

"That's what everyone keeps telling us, but I know my husband. He wouldn't just sit and wait if there was any chance of getting out. It's been too long. We need to go find them."

Old Red laughed again. "That so? Well, don't let me stop you. You'll have to hire a sled team though, cause nobody's flying right now. But if you decide to wait till it clears up, I can take you out there."

"You have a bush plane?"

"Damn right, I do, best ever built. It's a Norseman, a big Pratt & Whitney R-1340, 650 horsepower motor, and built back in 1937 when they knew how."

"Can it take all of us?"

"Sure, she can. She's a good old bird and I just put the skis on her, too. Might need a little maintenance first, but it's not like we're goin anywhere tonight, anyway, so you might as well relax. If you plan on hiring me you can start by buying me another beer."

Karen leaned forward and looked him in the eyes. "No more beer. You're leaving here with us, right now. You are going to sober up and get that airplane of yours ready to fly so you can take us to that secret lake of yours as soon as this weather breaks."

"Now you just hold on a goldarn minute there. Where do you get off trying to tell me what to do? I'll leave here when I'm good and ready."

"Then get ready. Or all your buddies here are going to see the two of us drag your sorry drunk ass out of here. So do you want to come along peacefully, or not?"

Old Red scowled at them then suddenly busted out laughing. "I heard you was a spitfire." He looked around the room and got a big grin on his face. He shouted out, so everyone could hear him. "All right, if you ladies insist that I accompany you, I shall." Heads turned in their direction. "See boys, Old Red's still got it. Let's go, girls. Gonna have a hot time tonight!"

Whistles and cheers followed. Karen felt the color rise on her face, both in anger and embarrassment. Pattie and Karen each took an arm to help Old Red stand and received more cheers and clapping, which followed them as they went out the door.

"Dear Lord, you stink!" Pattie said as they made their way over to her car.

Jamie opened the back door and got out. "Is that him?"

"Hey there, young fella. So, you've heard of me, too, have you?" He put a hand out.

Jamie covered his nose and took a step back. "No way. He is not riding in back with me."

"Wait, wait. What about my truck?" Old Red pointed at an old rusted-out blue Ford pickup truck barely visible under a thick blanket of snow. "I can't leave it here."

"You're in no shape to drive. Give me your keys," Karen ordered.

With a grimace, he dug in his pocket and handed them over.

"I'll drive him back to my house in his truck. You and Jamie can follow me."

Jamie hung back while the two women swept empty beer cans off the passenger seat and then helped Old Red get in. When they closed the door, Red slumped against the window.

Together Pattie and Karen cleared snow off the truck's front and back windows so that Karen could see to drive. She opened the driver's door and immediately covered her nose. "Ugh, looks like I'm going to have to keep the windows cracked."

"Sorry about that." Pattie grimaced in sympathy. "Thanks for taking him. We'll get him cleaned up when we get back."

Karen nodded. "Hope he doesn't put up too much of a fight. I also hope that airplane of his works."

"Did he say it was built in 1937? That's old."

"Well, look at him. He's really old too." They both frowned at the smelly bedraggled man lying against the window. He started snoring.

"So is this truck." Pattie shook her head. "Hope the heater works, plus the radio so you can drown him out."

"Let's hope." Karen smiled. "Stay close and flash your lights if you need me to stop."

Karen wrestled with the old pick-up's stiff wheel, and its clunky manual transmission, but when she hit the accelerator the tires plowed through the snow drifts and tracked straight. The heater started to put out warm air after a mile or so and she managed not to stall the engine when changing gears. She was getting the feel of the vehicle and started to relax a bit until a moose suddenly appeared in the truck's headlights and she had to slam on the brakes. The truck fishtailed and she barely avoided spinning out. Pattie's car crunched to a stop behind her. The moose froze and stared, its eyes gleaming eerily in the truck's lights, then it turned its heavy antlered head away and continued its lumbering gait across the highway where it disappeared into the pines. With the window a quarter-down so that she could breathe free of Old Red's stink, she smelled the musky odor of the moose. She decided she preferred it to that of Old Red. She restarted the engine and drove on. The snow fell in white sheets and blew in through the open window, defeating the best efforts of the truck's heater. She had to stop several times to free the windshield wipers when they froze up. Old Red snored through it all and, unfortunately, the radio didn't work.

Once safely back in Karen's driveway, she and Pattie wrestled him out of the Ford and half-carried him into the house. Jamie stood back out of the way and watched them with a look of amazed revulsion.

"Let's set him at the kitchen table and I'll put on some coffee," Karen said. Before going for the coffee she pulled out a can of pine-scented air freshener and dosed the area liberally. Old Red looked around the room, blearily oblivious to her efforts to combat his aroma.

"Bet he hasn't had a bath in a week," said Pattie.

"More like a month," Jamie commented. "Why would Dad trust this guy?"

Karen didn't have an answer for that. "I don't know. Maybe we can figure it out after we get some coffee in him and sober him up."

After two pots of coffee and a bowl of beef stew, Old Red started to come around, enough so that he was trying to flirt with her and Pattie. When he pinched Karen's butt, her son burst out laughing.

"Jamie, it's past your bedtime. Say goodnight." Karen told him.

"What? No. This is just getting good."

"Don't give me any more trouble," she warned. "Not tonight!"

He rolled his eyes, sighed, and went upstairs. Once he was out of earshot, she turned back to Old Red. "Now, as for you, Casanova, it's time to clean up your act," Karen adopted the same stern manner she used for Jamie and pointed down the hall. "You need to get yourself into that back bathroom over there and take a shower. Throw your clothes out the door. Wash yourself head to toe, and use soap, and I mean lots of it. Don't come out until you're squeaky clean. I'll wash your old clothes and find you something to wear in the meantime."

"Fine. I'll go take a shower if you want me to, but only under one condition. You gals take it with me." Red winked at her.

Pattie's eyes widened at Karen, waiting for it.

Karen knew he wasn't completely sober, but even so, it was hard to believe that he could think he was attractive to them or anyone else with eyes or a nose. Time to set him straight. "Let me tell you this very clearly. You smell like over-ripe road kill. You are getting into that shower, one way or another. You can either do it on your own, or we will join you and take a wire brush to you that'll take your hide off along with the dirt."

He stopped smiling. "You're kind of a hard woman, aren't you? No wonder Jimmy couldn't wait to go fishing."

Karen felt her rage soar. She got to her feet and pointed at the bathroom. "Go. Take. A. Shower. Now!"

"Okay, okay." Red stood and backed away from her, grumbling and stumbling as he headed down the hall toward the bathroom. "Don't have to get all pissy with me. I was just funning. You got no sense of humor. None at all."

When Red started throwing clothes out the bathroom door, Karen put on her dishwashing gloves to pick them up. One plaid flannel shirt, one pair of grey dungarees, grungy long johns, and socks of indeterminate color. She turned her head away and carried them by her fingertips. She threw them all into the washing machine with a double load of soap and bleach.

The bathroom door opened again, and a dirty old baseball cap flew out. Pattie went to retrieve it. "Be careful with that, it's my lucky hat." One of Red's eyes peered at her through the cracked door. "Can't fly without it."

"Trust me," Pattie replied, "Your hat's safe with us."

"Better be." The door closed, and the water came on.

"He is one weird dude," Pattie said and handed the hat over to Karen.

Karen frowned at the greasy old thing. "Guess I better wash this by hand. I don't want to give him any excuses."

***

Red slept off the last of his beer in Karen's guest room. When he came out the next morning, he was still hung over but looked like a different person, at least ten years younger, dressed in clean if newly bleach-faded clothing. His long hair was combed and tied back, and his beard was trimmed short and neat. He sat at the oak kitchen table and Karen put a cup of hot coffee in front of him plus a couple of aspirin. He swallowed the aspirin dry and stared at the cup.

Red said "There was a time though when folks respected me. I was one of the best bush pilots and big game guides around. People came from all over the world to fly with me. I got writ up in the papers even."

"So what happened?" Pattie asked.

Red shrugged and gave her a half-smile. "The usual. Life. Death. Money. Lost a lot of business staying home to take care of my wife. Then I had to sell the house to pay off the medical bills after she passed. No one to go home to, no home to go home to. Guess I just didn't care anymore and started drinkin' too much."

Karen asked, "Now the question is, can you stay sober long enough to help us find our husbands?"

Old Red nodded. "I know those mountains better than most anybody. I'll fly out there and look for them."

"Is this plane of yours in any condition to fly? Because you certainly weren't."

He narrowed his eyes at her, and his voice took on an angry defensive tone again. "I may not be much good at taking care of myself, Missy, but I take real good care of my plane. She'll fly."

"Okay. And do you think you can find this secret lake of yours again?"

"I don't think, I know."

"Good. How soon can you be ready to go?"

"I'm ready now, but I have to wait till the weather clears like everybody else. I ain't no magician."

"Understood. And how many people will your plane hold?"
"Ten. Why?"

"We're coming with you," Karen said.

He met her eyes again, a look of surprise. "Both of you?"

"Yes. And my fourteen-year-old son Jamie. That will give us four pairs of eyes to search. And we'll need survival gear for all of us, plus our husbands. Do you have enough on hand, or do we need to go shopping?"

"No. I got plenty. I'll provide the gear. You don't have to pay me, but you will have to pay for the gas."

"Agreed."

Chapter 10
The Sheep Trail

November 2, 1973

The trail they'd found appeared well-used. It had probably been made by the native Big Horn Dall Sheep, but its current width indicated that bigger animals had been using it as well. It was wide enough for Jim to walk alongside Ronnie and help support him. Best of all, it was leading them downward. They pressed on following the switchbacks as the trail snaked back and forth down the mountain. The snow fell steadily, but they were sheltered from the wind by the overhanging cliffs above. With Jim's support, Ronnie kept limping ahead, but every so often, he had to stop.

"Oh man, I don't know how much further I can go." He stood on his good leg, holding himself up with his arm on Jim's shoulder. His teeth were bared in a grimace of pain.

"Just rest a moment." Jim steadied Ronnie as he helped him lean back against the rocky cliff at his back.

A cold gust of wind swirled up from below and blew the snow aside long enough to give them a glimpse of what lay below…a tree-filled slope down to a long flat valley.

"Look. This trail is taking us down into those trees in that valley," Jim said. "That forest doesn't look all that much further. We should be there in less than an hour."

"Man, I hope so." After a few more minutes of rest, Ronnie nodded his readiness and they went on, slowly working their way down the rocky trail. It took more than Jim's guestimate of an hour, partly because it was further than he'd thought, but mostly because Ronnie needed frequent rest stops. The first sign they'd reached the forest was a slender pine tree appearing in front of them. "I've never been so glad to see a tree in my life."

Here the trail left the protection of the cliff walls and disappeared under the snow. The trees increased in number and they found themselves slogging through deep drifts again. The icy wind swirled around the trees, throwing snow in their faces. To keep from slipping and sliding out of control, they had to stay parallel to the steep terrain, taking it slow, and changing direction frequently as needed to crisscross the steep snow-covered hillside and stay upright in the process as they fought against the bitterly cold wind. Many times, they had to backtrack to get through the thick growth. Exhausted, they collapsed with their backs against the trunk of a huge pine tree taking refuge on its leeward side to get out of the wind. Visibility was no more than fifteen feet.

"Time to start thinking about making another shelter for the night," Jim said.

"Good idea." Ronnie sighed. "I'm wiped out. I couldn't have gone much further, and I have to admit your snow pit kept us warm enough last night. Where'd you learn to do that, anyway?"

"Old native trick."

"You part Eskimo or something?"

"Inuit," Jim corrected.

"Oh." Ronnie fell silent, evidently puzzled by Jim's shift in mood. Cautiously, after a full minute passed, he tried again. "So, you're part Inuit then?"

Jim sighed but decided to answer. He knew Ronnie meant well. "On my mother's side. Her father was a full-blooded Inuit. She taught me some of the old ways."

"Cool," Ronnie said.

"I have an idea. You rest here for a spell while I go find us a sheltered place for the night."

Jim stood and trudged into the dense forest. It didn't take him long to find what he was looking for. He went back to get Ronnie. "I found just the place. Let's get you over there."

Helping Ronnie to his feet and supporting him, they followed Jim's tracks through the thick forest where Jim stopped them at the base of a giant Fir tree. Its wide snow-laden branches touched the ground all around it.

"We're going to make camp under this tree here. I'm going to need that shovel again."

Jim helped Ronnie sit down to unstrap the shovel from his bad leg. "What's so special about this tree? Looks like all the others to me

"This one has a good-sized tree well that's not too deep."

"What's a tree well?"

"It's when the snow builds up around the windward side of a tree and creates a cave at the bottom. Deep ones are real dangerous if you slip in accidentally, especially head-first, but nice wide ones like this can make great shelters in an emergency."

Jim started digging. He soon created a slanted ditch going down below the overhanging branches which he kept aloft by propping them up with sticks. He piled the removed snow along the edges to build a protective wall. When he reached the bottom of the well, he found it filled with pine needles, a good start. He climbed out and worked on cutting boughs, making a pile of them next to Ronnie.

"We'll use these to trap warm air between us and the snow. Crawl inside and I'll hand them to you. We need to cover the entire floor and sides."

In all, it took them maybe thirty minutes to construct a cozy nest of pine boughs under the tree's overhanging branches. Once they settled inside their deep well-protected nest, they agreed it was the best shelter they'd had thus far.

A lit candle and their combined body heat soon warmed the cave to a comfortable level, warm enough to melt snow for a drink as they shared another piece of jerky.

"Thanks," Ronnie said, then laid down on the soft pine needles. "You think we'll make it back?"

"Course we will. Once we're down off this mountain we'll make better time. Meanwhile, let's get a good night's sleep and tomorrow we'll—" he stopped there seeing that Ronnie was already out, lost to exhausted sleep. Tomorrow would be a challenge he hoped they were up to.

Never give up, he told himself and pinched out the candle flame, leaving them in pitch black. As soon as he lay down next to Ronnie, sleep claimed him.

Sunlight filtering through the tree's branches woke Jim.

"Hey," Ronnie greeted him, already awake and sitting upright.

"I need to pee," Jim announced and crawled out of their nest. He trudged through the deep snow about ten paces away. As he stood and relieved himself, a hint of something dark moving, caught his eye. He tensed and stared for a long while into the shadows where the trees thickened. When he didn't see it again, he decided it must have just been shadows cast by branches swaying in the wind. He zipped up and went back to their shelter. Time for some breakfast, he thought, then they'd head out again.

As he came back, he saw Ronnie standing outside with the shovel strapped to his leg again. Ronnie's eyes flashed wide and he pointed behind Jim. "Bear! There's a bear."

Jim spun around, grabbing for the 44 magnum pistol in his chest holster. Before he completed the maneuver, sharp pain stabbed through his ribs, taking him to his knees. He gasped for breath but managed to point the gun in the direction Ronnie pointed. All he saw were dark trees and blowing snow. He sniffed the air and listened hard for the sounds of snuffling, growling, or branches breaking. If a bear was out there in the shadows, he could neither see nor hear nor smell it. Bears bore a rank odor that was hard to miss. "Where...where is it?"

"I don't know. It's gone now, but it was right over there, I swear. Come on, let's get out of here. Bears scare the shit out of me."

Jim pressed a hand against his ribs and got to his feet. "Yeah, okay, go ahead of me." He helped Ronnie up then walked sideways behind him, keeping watch. "Could you tell what kind it was? Black bear or grizzly?"

"I don't know, man, but it was big, really big, standing up on its hind legs, looking straight at us."

Ronnie limped ahead, moving faster than he had before even with Jim's assistance. Jim stayed close, holding his pistol and continually checking behind them. The swirling snow was creating a near whiteout so there was little he could see. After a while, the wind died down and the snow let up giving him visibility a few yards ahead and behind. With no sign of a bear, Jim put away his gun. As they moved down the slope, he scanned the forest floor for fallen branches hoping to spot one that would serve Ronnie as a crutch. He doubted his ribs could take much more abuse and knew they needed to move faster if there was any hope of getting off this mountain before sunset.

He'd like to get out of these thick woods where it was hard to see what might be waiting around the next tree. Once clear, he could take their bearings and aim them southwest. Down off the mountain, the odds of finding shelter would improve. Probably the best they'd find would be a hollowed-out tree or an abandoned cave. But there was also the longshot of coming across a cabin or a hunting lodge. If they were lucky, really lucky. He hoped they'd be that fortunate. He wasn't looking forward to digging snow pits every night and their meager rations would soon run out. A cabin might have food stored in it. If this were summer, they could catch fish, but it wasn't, and this sudden unexpected freeze no doubt froze over any nearby streams and lakes. Still, they had a shovel that could break through the ice and he had his pistol. The first rabbit or deer he spotted would be dinner.

A long, thick fallen branch caught his eye and he detoured to grab it. "Here, try this. It might help."

Ronnie took the branch and stabbed one end into the snow, holding on tight to the other as he stepped forward with his shovel-supported leg. "Yeah, that works. Thanks." He moved even faster now.

They were making good progress through the forest, which was less steep now and beginning to thin, suggesting they were nearing its edge. Through the trees, he saw an open field below and a frozen stream. He imagined breaking through the ice and using the fishing line and safety pin in Pattie's survival kit. He pointed ahead. "There's where we need to go."

"Hey, look at that. We're nearly outa here," Ronnie said, seeing now what Jim was pointing at.

Then Jim heard a loud metallic clang.

Ronnie screamed and went down.

Jim rushed to his side. A jagged-toothed bear trap gripped Ronnie's previously one good leg. Jim grabbed the sides of the steel trap and tried to force it open, but his ribs stabbed him in protest and he hadn't enough strength left.

"Get it off me!" Ronnie yelled.

"I'm trying. Give me that stick." He grabbed the branch, wedged it in, and tried to pry open the trap. The metal jaws held tight and the branch snapped in two. He pulled out his long hunting knife, and carefully slipped the flat side between the trap's teeth and Ronnie's leg, got the edge of his boot lined up along the other side, and then pushed and pulled with all his might, crying out in pain from his injured ribs. The steel jaws parted just enough for Ronnie to pull his foot out before Jim had to let go. The trap snapped shut again like a hungry shark, trapping his knife. Both men lay on their backs breathing hard and moaning from their pain.

"Are you…bleeding?" Jim asked between hard breaths.

"I don't know. I can't look."

Jim slowly sat up. He saw red soaking through the pant leg just above Ronnie's boot.

"How bad is it?" Ronnie asked, still lying flat on his back.

"Not so bad," he lied. "I'll just wrap it up like I did your other leg."

Ronnie propped himself up on his elbows to look. "Oh man, I am so screwed." He laid back down. "I'm never getting out of here now."

"You'll be fine," Jim said with conviction simply because he couldn't accept any other possibility. Once again, he pulled out Pattie's ridiculously inadequate survival kit. Another twelve feet of plastic wrap and a length of electrical tape were put to use. He pulled the pant leg back down over the plastic and stuffed Ronnie's rapidly swelling foot back into the boot before it became too puffy to fit. Ronnie cried out as Jim shoved the foot inside.

"Sorry." Jim laced the boot snugly to help prevent further swelling.

"That was a bear trap, right?"

"Right."

"Which means somebody around here thinks this is a good place to catch bears. Like the one I saw."

"So it seems. Let's get moving."

Ronnie looked at Jim incredulously. "And just how the hell am I going to do that? I've got two messed-up legs now."

"Yeah. You're a real pain in the ass."

"Fuck you."

Jim got to his feet. "Come on. Get onto my back."

"What? That's crazy. You can't carry me."

"Sure I can. You're skinny and we don't have that far to go before we're out of these woods. I'll feel better once we reach that stream. I'm thinking we can catch some fish."

"Fish, huh? That does sound good."

Jim crouched low and waited. When Ronnie grabbed him around his neck, he slowly stood, trying to balance so that the other man's weight was evenly distributed. The first step nearly took them both down. He shifted and tried again. *Better.* "There. I got you now."

He moved ahead, one plodding step at a time. He thanked the clearing skies above that the snow was only a foot deep here, further evidence that they were nearing the valley floor. In the lower elevations, the winds should be less wicked and the temperatures slightly warmer than they'd experienced so far. He'd put on a confident front for Ronnie that he could easily carry him. In truth, it would require every last bit of his remaining strength. The terrain was still uneven and downward-sloping, forcing him to choose his footing carefully as he made his way through the trees. He kept going even when it reached the point that he thought he couldn't.

One more step, just get past one more tree, nearly there, come on, keep going, gotta keep going.

Ronnie grunted as Jim fell forward onto his hands and knees. Speckled darkness swam in front of his eyes, he'd come close to passing out.

Ronnie rolled off to lie on his back. "That's it, man. You can't carry me any further and I can't walk. I'm done for."

Jim laid down next to him. "Just need to rest a minute. We're almost there."

"You mean we're almost nowhere and the sunlight's nearly gone. That valley down there's probably not much better than right here anyway."

"It should be warmer down there. Less wind, too."

"Maybe."

Jim didn't have the strength to argue and Ronnie wasn't wrong. They were well below where they'd camped last night so that was an improvement. If he could get a fire going, this spot was probably as good as any to spend the night. "Okay. Fine, we'll camp here."

When he got his breath back, Jim borrowed the shovel from Ronnie's leg again and cleared away a circle of snow to reveal the hard, frozen earth beneath. There was no tree well to dig down into, but he could build a wall up and around. His arms felt like rubber, along with his legs, but he kept working. Soon packed snow enclosed the perimeter. He then gathered pine boughs again to build a raised floor to insulate them from the cold ground. With fallen branches and more pine boughs, he created a lean-to shelter from the falling snow that helped to trap body heat. He filled the trash bag from Pattie's survival kit with fallen pine needles and twigs for kindling, carried it back, and dumped it out in front of their tiny campsite. The dry needles and twigs quickly caught fire, burning hot and bright, but didn't last long, so he piled more on to keep the flames going until the thicker branches finally stopped smoldering and caught fire as well. He soon had a decent campfire in front of their shelter radiating heat into it.

No sign of the moon yet, but the stars were coming out, silver dots piercing a velvety deep-blue sky as the clouds moved on. The wind stilled, and it was a relief not to have snow blowing at them for a change, but clear skies correlated with rapidly dropping temperatures. It would be cold tonight, maybe the coldest they had experienced since leaving Anchorage. Without this fire, they'd be in serious trouble. Ronnie shivered, and his teeth chattered, even with his hands extended toward the flames.

"Put this on." Jim ripped a hole at the end of the trash bag and slipped it over Ronnie's head.

"What about you?" Ronnie asked.

"I'm warm enough." Another lie told well.

The two men huddled under the lean-to, facing the small fire, feeding it continuously. The heat in their faces and chests was soon almost too hot to bear, but the icy cold still seeped through the backs of their heavy parkas and Ronnie's extra layer of plastic.

Together, they polished off the last Snicker's bar and chewed on another ration of the tough beef jerky. Silhouetted in the dark, Ronnie's body enveloped inside the black plastic bag became invisible. Between his dark watch cap and scarf, only his upper face showed in the firelight.

Jim saw Ronnie's eyes droop, and his head bobbing.

"Lie down. Get some rest," Jim told him. "We'll take turns tending the fire."

Ronnie nodded, laid down, and was soon sound asleep. Jim decided there'd be no sleep for him. Too dangerous. He needed to stay awake and keep the fire going. Occasionally he stood to stamp his feet and slap his hands to keep his circulation going, but his tired legs ached so that he couldn't do it for long and had to sit back down.

The dark hours crawled by. The bright stars gradually made their way across the black sky, a slow backward-moving celestial clock. He noted the location of the North Star directly above with the tale of the Small Dipper pointing it out and recognized the Big Dipper lower to the right. That meant the valley below them lay southwest, the direction they needed to go. The town of Talkeetna was also southwest, but a lot further away. About a hundred miles, he estimated. Minutes by plane. Weeks on foot.

Between here and there might be summer hunting lodges and winter cabins. The hunting lodges frequented by tourists would be empty now, of course, but bush people lived in their cabins year-round. The trick was finding one. He shook his head at the thought. They had a better chance of being struck by lightning. No, the real trick here would be staying alive long enough to walk out in winter without any supplies to speak of. Not even his hardy Inuit ancestors would have signed up for this. He nearly laughed but didn't have the energy for it.

He was so damned tired. Just a little while longer, then he'd have to wake Ronnie, turn the fire-tending over to him, and get some sleep. That was his last thought before his eyes closed.

Chapter 11
The Bear

November 4, 1973

Sunlight pierced through the tree branches dancing over Jim as his eyelids opened. The fire was out, buried in snow, and he was lying on his side, ice cold and his body ached all over. His mind slowly registered where he was. He must have fallen asleep sometime during the long night and was lucky to have woken at all.

"Ronnie!" he yelled in sudden fear and pushed himself up despite the pain of blood rushing back into nearly frozen limbs. He shook Ronnie who lay next to him covered in the heavy trash bag. When Ronnie moaned in protest, a tremendous sense of relief washed over him. Not dead. He hadn't failed him. Not yet. "Wake up. Ronnie, I need you to wake up."

Ronnie's eyes opened and blinked at him. "We're still alive?"

"Must be because I hurt all over. How about you?"

Ronnie tried to sit up, moaned, and fell back, squeezing his eyes shut. "My leg's on fire and the rest of me feels like I'm being stabbed with icicles."

The stabbing part was fine, that was just blood circulating back into chilled extremities. The *on-fire* part wasn't. "Let me take a look." Jim carefully lifted Ronnie's pant legs. The broken leg didn't look much different than before. The one the rusty old bear trap got yesterday showed a thin red line extending an inch above the boot top. *Blood poisoning.* Fatal if it reaches the heart or any other vital organ. The only cure he knew was penicillin.

"It's infected, isn't it?" Ronnie said, watching Jim's face.

Jim nodded. Walking would make it worse but lying here waiting for help to arrive wasn't an option. No one was coming. He pulled out Pattie's survival kit and fished out two aspirin. "Take these. No argument."

With Jim's help, Ronnie sat up. He reached for the foil dish in which they had melted snow the previous night, but the water had re-frozen, so he swallowed the aspirin down dry, making a face as he did so.

"I'll get the fire going again and we'll get warmed up. Have something to eat."

With the fire relit Jim prepared a concoction of pine needles steeped in boiling snow water. Ronnie watched him without comment. The fact that Ronnie had no sarcasm to offer wasn't a good sign. They sat near the fire feeling both the pleasure and pain of rewarming themselves and shared a meager breakfast— another strip of beef jerky each, and an oatmeal cookie broken in two. They passed the foil bowl filled with steaming pine-needle tea, back and forth, and chewed slowly despite ravenous hunger, savoring each crumb as if it were their last.

"When we're done, we'll head out again and see how far we can get," Jim said.

Ronnie swallowed the last of his cookie and shook his head. "No, I'll wait here. You'll make better time on your own."

Jim let out a long deep sigh. "We already went over this."

"Look. I got two bad legs now and there's no way you can keep carrying me."

"Sure I can. That valley's not far now. You can see it from here."

"Yeah, I see it, and it's almost straight down. As I said, there's no way."

Jim carefully refolded the foil bowl and packed it along with their remaining food and matches into his pockets. He got to his feet and gestured toward the boulder Ronnie leaned against. "If you can get your ass on top of that rock, it'll be easier for me to lift you onto my back."

"Forget it, man. Stop trying to be the big hero. You need to go on without me." Ronnie stayed put, hands outstretched to the fire. "I can get around enough to keep this fire going till you get back with help. I'll be fine."

"No, you won't. Leaving you here isn't an option. So either do as I say or I'm going to drag your ass down this mountain anyway. It would be easier on us both if you cooperated, but either way, you're not staying here. So, what's it going to be?"

Frowning, Ronnie shook his head but crawled atop the rock and got up onto his knees. "You're crazy, you know that."

"No argument." Jim turned his back and crouched low for Ronnie to grab hold, then slowly stood. "Okay. I got you."

"Yeah, you keep saying that."

Jim smiled. The sarcastic tone was back. He started to work his way through the trees as more snow fell and swirled around them. The heavy cloud cover had moved in again. He went slow, keeping to the middle, careful to avoid slipping into a tree well. Through branches, he caught glimpses of the valley below, a wide expanse of level snow-covered ground. He fervently hoped he wasn't hallucinating, though it was a likely conclusion. He felt lightheaded from lack of food and exposure, combined with the constant ache and occasional jab from his injured ribs. The added weight of carrying Ronnie was sapping what reserves he had left. He was strong, but he wasn't Superman. He focused on each step, working his way downward. He'd know if the level terrain he saw ahead was real or imagined soon enough.

Ronnie lapsed into silence, riding semi-consciously on his back. Jim kept moving slogging through snow, pausing every so often to catch his breath for a moment, then continuing downward again for what felt like hours. The trees gradually thinned as the slope gentled and finally turned into level terrain. Snow still fell heavily around them so that he couldn't see more than twenty feet ahead. His back was breaking, and his ribs screamed in agony.

"I gotta set you down," Jim wheezed and carefully lowered Ronnie to the ground. The effort took the last of his strength and he fell onto all fours.

"You okay?" Ronnie asked.

Jim could only shake his head and wheeze in answer.

"Take your time. It's not like I'm going anywhere." Ronnie scoffed then looked past Jim and cried out. "Bear! It's that freaking bear again!"

Jim rolled to his back, his gun half-drawn when he froze, looking into the barrel of a rifle pointed directly at his face. He lifted his gaze to take in the fearsome creature that held it, something that looked for all intents like a giant grizzly. Then the bear spoke.

"Don't move or I'll blow your goddamn head off."

Jim let the pistol drop back into its holster and raised his hands to show empty palms. Only now did he see the man inside the bearskin. Jim estimated the stranger stood at least six foot six and weighed around three hundred pounds. He wore a bear's hide with the forelegs as sleeves and the hind legs draped behind with its long black claws reaching the ground. The bear's head formed a hood that partially obscured the man's face. A scruffy red and grey beard covered the rest, blending in with the fur. From any distance at all, one would see only a bear standing on its hind legs, preparing to attack. A string of small animals hung over the man's fur-covered shoulder which backed up one very old, very large caliber rifle pointed at Jim's head.

"Take it easy, Mister," Jim said. "We don't want any trouble."

"Then you shouldn't have come here."

Jim kept his arms raised and his body still. "It's not like we planned it. We're stranded, half-frozen, and half-starved. We're no threat to anyone. Who are you? Where did you come from?"

"Name's Elijah, Elijah Thaddeus Boone. This here's my valley and you be trespassin'." Elijah squinted over the barrel, studying him.

"We didn't mean to," Jim stated, hoping this man behind the rifle wasn't as crazy as he appeared. "We crashed in the mountains, and our plane burned up taking all our gear with it."

"Zat so? Saw you fellas comin down my trail. Been followin you most of the day—wonderin where you was headed, how you found your way in here. First time anybody's made it this far since I been here. This place don't allow it. But here you are, ain't ya? Bleedin all over the place, lyin half-dead on my doorstep. Now, it looks like I got to decide what to do with the both of ya."

"Please. We're just trying to get home to our families."

Elijah paused, and the rifle dipped ever so slightly, enough that Jim no longer stared directly into the open barrel. "Family, huh?"

Still lying on his back, Jim nodded, hopeful now. "Yes. Our wives. And my son. He just turned fourteen."

The big man glanced aside before looking back. "Had a son myself once. A long time ago. You fellas are my first visitors since I come here—not that I ever wanted any, mind ya. Don't know why you were let in, but … I don't know…maybe it's a sign, you showin' up here now." Elijah took a step back, turned the rifle around, and balanced it on his shoulder. He rubbed a leather-wrapped hand across his mouth. "Guess we're gonna find out, ain't we?"

Jim didn't know how to respond to that. He didn't want to either contradict this man or feed into his delusions, so he chose silence and lay there waiting for Elijah to speak again.

Instead, the big man turned around in a slow circle, nodding to the forest and surrounding mountains. When he completed the circle, he faced the tallest peak and yelled out. "Alright then. That's how you want it, that's how it'll be." He returned his gaze to Jim and Ronnie at his feet, and a large grin lit up his face.

"Now that that's decided, I reckon I better get you boys back to my place so we can patch you up." He winked at Ronnie, who stared back with an open mouth. "Look at you, boy. You're just a little feller. No wonder your friend here could carry you even though he's hurt bad, too." Elijah turned to Jim. "Don't think you could carry him much further though. Wait here while I make transportation arrangements."

Chapter 12
Elijah takes them home

November 4, 1973

Jim and Ronnie gaped at this monster of a man as he trudged back into the woods, hardly believing there was someone there who could help them. Assuming he intended to. Hermit bush people were often wackos and this guy seemed to be one of them.

"Is he coming back?" Ronnie asked.

Jim sat up and shrugged. "I don't know. Let's hope so. Because he's right. I'm spent. And I have no idea where we are. I keep checking my compass but look what it's doing." He held it out for Ronnie to see. The needle spun, never stopping. "I have no idea where to go from here. Can't see the sun either."

The heavy clouds diffused the sunlight so that the entire sky was evenly lit to a soft pale yellow. "Need to rest awhile. We'll wait and see if he comes back. If not, we'll make camp," Jim said. Ronnie offered no counter plan. After an hour, maybe more? Amazingly, Jim realized it wasn't all that cold sitting here. "It's warmer," he announced, surprised even though he'd predicted it.

Ronnie followed his lead, looking up in surprise when his bare palm touched down. "You're right. Wonder why."

"Mountains block the wind down here," Elijah replied coming out of the forest and dragging something large behind him. "If you'd gone down the other side, you would a slid down a glacier and be frozen by now." He stopped in front of them and proudly displayed his creation…a sled of sorts, made up of a series of branches lashed closely together between two long poles peeled free of bark.

"Where'd you find that?" Ronnie asked.

"Didn't find it. I made it. This is a travois, a drag-sled. You boys are going to lie on it and take a ride back to my place."

"You sure you can pull us both? Ronnie might be a lightweight, but I'm not. Add us together and that's over 400 pounds," Jim said.

"Yeah, I figured as much. Which is why I'm not the one who's gonna be doin the pullin. He is!" Elijah gestured his left hand behind him. A huge brown bear hidden in the swirling snow and shadows of the pines, snuffled forward. It sniffed the air and then let out a tremendous roar. Jim reached for his pistol, but Elijah booted him. "None of that now. He won't hurt you… long as you follow the rules of course."

Elijah set down his trapped animals and gun, faced the bear, and walked toward it. The huge animal lifted onto its back legs as Elijah approached.

"Oh man," Ronnie said under his breath. "He's a goner. Get ready with that pistol."

Jim snuck his hand into his jacket and wrapped it around the gun's handle. The rest of him remained still. He didn't want to draw the bear's attention, knowing it could cover the distance between them in a heartbeat.

Standing upright, the bear towered above Elijah, who kept walking toward it. Jim braced himself to witness the carnage. Elijah reached out to the bear and its huge clawed forearms wrapped around him. The bear opened its mouth taking Elijah's head inside its jaws, but there were no hideous screams. Instead, Elijah chuckled, and the bear made muffled noises much like a dog greeting its master, and continued to mouth the man without drawing blood.

"I'll be damned," Ronnie said. "They're buds."

"Come on now, Griz. I need your help," Elijah said to the bear and pushed away. The bear dropped to all fours. Elijah dragged the travois over to the bear and placed one end atop the bear's back then lashed the two long poles in place with rawhide straps. He tested to make sure the drag-sled held in place, then guided the bear over to where Ronnie and Jim sat watching in stunned amazement.

Elijah bent down and lifted Ronnie as if he were a child and laid him onto the travois. He gestured at Jim. "There's room for you, too. Climb aboard."

"No thanks. I'll walk," Jim insisted and pushed himself up to his feet, grimacing in pain.

"Sure, about twenty feet afore you fall on your face. Don't argue. They's the rules."

When the deep breath he took to do just that, stabbed through his chest so sharply that he gasped instead, Jim recognized the truth of Elijah's observation. He wouldn't get more than twenty feet. "Fine." He lowered himself down gingerly to lie next to Ronnie.

Elijah picked up his string of animals and the big rifle again then waved the bear forward. "Home, Grizzy."

The beast started through the woods. Elijah followed behind, taking long strides.

"Got a shortcut. Faster than goin along my trap line by the river."

"So that was one of your traps I stepped in?" Ronnie asked.

Elijah nodded. "Fraid so. T'weren 't meant for you though."

Jim grimaced with every bump bringing sharp pain shooting through his torso. Still, it was a big improvement over trudging down a mountainside with Ronnie on his back.

Lying here looking backward at Elijah, Jim couldn't see what lay ahead, but from what stretched out behind them this appeared to be a well-worn path, evidently made by human travel. But he saw no evidence of a cabin or other sign of civilization. Despite his pain, he lifted onto an elbow and twisted around to look ahead. What he saw was the rock face of a blind canyon, a dead end. He laid back and lifted his eyebrows in question at Elijah, but the man merely grinned back and kept walking.

When they reached the vertical granite wall, the bear stopped. Elijah unlashed the travois from the bear's back and lowered it onto the ground. Relieved of his burden, the bear turned back and stood next to the two men lying there. They held very still, their hearts pounding in their ears as the gigantic head swung inches above them, the black nose snuffling. This male was huge even by Grizzly standards. The width of the head exceeded the length of Jim's upper torso. Some part of his brain that was still functioning in this moment of pure terror wondered if it was a Kodiak but they normally only lived on that one island and that was a long way away from here. The beast rocked his head and then bellowed, opening his mouth to display long sharp teeth and spew stinking bear breath. Ronnie cried out and Jim cringed. Seemingly satisfied that he'd made his point, the bear closed his mouth, grunted then turned away and lumbered back down the trail he'd come by.

"He likes you," Elijah said. "Rides over though. We got to walk in from here." Elijah lifted Ronnie into his arms again. Jim painfully pushed himself to his feet.

"Can you make it?" Elijah asked.

Jim nodded. "Yeah, I'll make it."

"Good. Stay close. It's easy to get lost in here." Then he disappeared behind a huge boulder.

Startled by the seeming vanishing act, Jim hurried forward and found a cleft in the wall, maybe three feet wide. He walked through and found Elijah waiting around a curve.

"I said, stay close," Elijah ordered then moved ahead with Ronnie. Jim followed him on a narrow path lightly dusted in snow that cut through the towering cliffs. The passage twisted and turned upon itself like a maze with frequent side openings leading off in other directions. Jim stayed close, recognizing the danger of getting lost. Eventually, Elijah led him down a path that opened up into another canyon. This canyon was narrower than the outer one, about the width of a football field, with smooth vertical walls shooting up hundreds of feet all around. Thick billowing white clouds blocked the entire sky. The further into the canyon they went, the stranger things became. The air warmed to a comfortable spring day, and large-leaved plants sprouted up everywhere he looked, reminding him of photos he'd seen of tropical islands.

They came upon a clearing with a carefully tended garden of brightly colored vegetables in long even rows and a grove of citrus trees. Citrus! ...in Alaska? The heavy snowfall ended abruptly almost as if they'd passed through an invisible barrier. Ahead, he saw something glittering. Water? Was that an actual stream flowing? He stopped and stood there staring about in disbelief.

"Ronnie, are you seeing what I'm seeing?"

When Ronnie didn't answer, he grew alarmed and rushed to catch up with Elijah.

"He's not doing so good," Elijah said. "Passed out awhile back."

Jim looked ahead. "That can't be running water, can it?"

"Sure looks like it to me," Elijah said. "Can't believe your eyes, can ya? Felt the same way the first time I saw this place."

As they got closer, Jim saw it truly was a stream running past the trees and garden down through the center of the canyon. Walking along the gurgling water, they soon came upon the source, a deep blue-green pond, ice-free with steam coming off its surface.

"Hot springs?" Jim asked.

Elijah nodded. "Underground springs. Keeps this whole canyon warm year-round."

"Wow." Jim had a million questions about how that worked. After all, even in Yellowstone Park with all its hot pools and famous geysers, snow still fell in the winter. What was keeping it out? "Must be more going on here than just hot springs."

"Save your questions for later. I got sickness to deal with first."

With still no sign of a cabin anywhere, Jim thought they were going to bed down in the open. After several hundred more yards they reached the end of the canyon, another vertical wall of granite, but this one had something else Jim never expected to see—a small wooden door embedded in the rock face.

The hand-carved wooden door hung from a heavy pole frame and was equipped with a wooden latch. Elijah flipped the latch aside, opened the door, bent over, and entered the mountain with Ronnie. Ducking to pass through the entrance, Jim found himself in a large circular cave.

"Welcome to my home," Elijah said. "Yours too now."

A pale green light coming through slots cut into the rock walls illuminated the interior revealing the space and furnishings within. In the strange green glow, Jim made out a cavern approximately twenty by thirty feet with a large domed ceiling. Sections of wood planking lay like decking over a natural stone floor with animal hides and sheepskins strewn about for rugs. Water trickled down the far back wall. Jim noted a four-poster bed, a long table with chairs, a cabinet, and a counter with a wooden sink, all hand-hewn from the local pines. Elijah gently lowered Ronnie down on the bed and propped his broken leg up on a pillow, then walked around lighting candles. The golden light counteracted the eerie green emanating from the walls. The cave felt pleasantly warm despite the absence of a fire, warm enough that Jim tugged off his parka. He sniffed the air.

"Why does it smell like lemons in here?" he asked.

"I put it in the candles, reminds me of my wife," Elijah said and bent over Ronnie as he lay there semi-conscious.

"Now let's take a look at those hurt legs o' yours. Those bear traps have some mighty strong springs."

He quieted as he examined Ronnie's bloodied ankle and the red streaks climbing up the calf. "Well, don't think it's broke, but we'll have to clean it up and get some of my cure-alls in you to fight this bad blood. I seen worse! Now the other leg's broke for sure. I'll need to set it and brace it. Don't you worry none, I done it before. Gonna hurt like hell o'course but needs doin. You won't be dancing no jig for a while, but you'll heal." Elijah positioned himself at the foot of the bed and took hold of Ronnie's broken leg at the ankle with both hands. "Your job is to grab that bed rail above your head and hold on tight."

"What? Wait, wait!" Ronnie screamed.

Jim interrupted. "You sure you know what you're doing?"

"Don't reckon you boys got any choice but to trust that I do. Now hold onto that rail, son, and it'll all be over in a coon's minute."

Elijah waited. Jim nodded reluctantly, and Ronnie reached up and grabbed the railing. Elijah gave a mighty pull, Ronnie let out a scream and then passed out, but Jim could see that the leg was set straight. He watched Elijah's thorough and careful ministrations as he cleaned and bandaged both legs, then braced the broken one with a smooth flat board that served the purpose far better than the shovel ever had. It seemed this Elijah did know what he was doing.

Jim stood beside Ronnie, waiting for him to come around. Elijah busied himself near the kitchen area, opening and shutting cabinet doors, pulling things out, chopping and mixing, and such.

When Ronnie opened his eyes, he moaned in pain. "What the hell did you let him do to me?"

"Sorry, son. Had to be done," Elijah said from across the room then came toward them with a pair of wooden mugs in his hands. "Here, this'll help." He handed Ronnie a mug. "That there's my special remedy for whatever ails ya. Takes away the pain and starts the healing. Based on an old recipe my granny gave me." He handed the second mug to Jim. "I figured you could use some too. Must be hurtin' pretty bad the way you're carryin' yourself. Broke ribs, I reckon."

Holding the wooden mug, Jim felt the warmth of the drink in his hands. He sniffed the aroma cautiously. Like the candles, it too smelled of lemons. He and Ronnie held their cups, neither man drinking.

Elijah slapped his knee and bellowed a laugh. "You boys, think I'd go to all this trouble just to poison you? I coulda shot you in the woods and left you for dead. You must think I'm dumb as hell or just plain crazy."

"No, I …," Jim said. He didn't want to offend their rescuer, but he wasn't ready to trust him completely either. "Truth is I don't know what to think. This is all so strange."

Elijah nodded, and his smile faded. "You don't know the half of it. But I'm thinkin' you fellers need to be layin' down for a spell afore I fill you in. If you trust me enough to drink that, I promise it'll help, but it's up to you. Do what you like. Meanwhile, I'll go rustle us up some food and we can talk later."

Jim decided trust was their best, perhaps their only option, and took an experimental sip from the cup. The hot liquid tasted almost exactly like lemon tea, but with a touch of spice, he didn't recognize. Whatever it was, it tasted good and warmed him all the way down.

"I think it's safe enough," he said to Ronnie who was watching him closely.

Ronnie drank the potion as well then laid back on the fur-covered bed. Jim stretched out next to him and covered himself with a soft blanket of fur. Exhausted from their exertions and painful injuries, and now under the influence of Granny's 'cure-all' medicine, the two men soon fell asleep in the warmth and apparent safety of Elijah's very peculiar cave in an even more peculiar valley.

Chapter 13
Flying with Old Red

November 4, 1973

Stone-cold sober for the first time in what may have been years, Old Red drove his rusty blue pickup out to his tie-down spot on Lake Hood, closely followed by a Chevy Blazer. Inside it was the two women who'd kidnapped him from The Birdhouse nearly a week ago. They hadn't let him out of their sight since.

Jamie sat in the backseat of Pattie's Blazer, his mom in the front passenger seat, with Pattie at the wheel. A high-pressure ridge had finally moved into the area and the weather over Anchorage was clear and cold, which meant planes could take off. Finally, they could go search for his dad.

The Blazer followed Red as he drove around the lake and stopped in front of a massive yellow airplane. Pattie parked behind the pickup and everyone inside bailed out.

"Wow," Jamie exclaimed, "that thing's twice as big as Dad's Cessna."

"Yeah, it is," said Karen, squinting at the plane suspiciously. She was looking hard, but she couldn't see anything wrong with it. "Hmmm…surprising. It looks like it's in good condition."

"Red did say he takes better care of his airplane than himself," Pattie replied.

The airplane sat on a giant set of skis securely tied down to the frozen lake and was wrapped with wing, tail, and windshield covers, plus a large thick insulated blanket over the big engine.

Jamie pointed at electrical cables running from a small shed out to the airplane. "Those are to power the heaters in the engine compartment and cockpit to keep everything from freezing. Dad has the same set-up."

The women stood back and watched Red methodically remove each of the covers then start his walk-around inspections. Jamie followed Red's footsteps, peppering him with questions about different parts of the aircraft. Together, he and the old man checked the fuel and oil levels, including the auxiliary tank in the cabin.

Jamie poked his head out the cabin door. "He's got an extra 40 gallons of fuel in here. Should be way more than we need."

"That's good. So how does everything else look?" Karen asked,

"Dad showed me what to check during a preflight inspection, and this old bird seems to be in very good shape."

Jamie went back to helping Red. Together they carried supplies out from the shed: survival gear, two large duffle bags, six sleeping bags, a rifle and shotgun, and three small tents. "I had all this stuff for my clients when I was still guiding big game hunters," Red told Karen and Pattie as he walked past. He and Jamie stowed the gear in the cargo hold at the rear of the cabin. Karen peered inside the cavernous interior and saw ten seats including the pilots.

"He seems to know what he's doing," remarked Pattie, who stood next to her looking inside.

"He does," agreed Karen, "Have to say I feel a little better now that we've seen his plane. I was pretty worried with the drunk we brought home, but he's obviously in his element, and has been doing it for a long time."

"I was talking about your son."

"Oh." She fell silent, feeling a little guilty now.

Red went to the front of the plane and pulled the prop around. "Nine revolutions, one for each cylinder. Have to do this with these big radial engines to prevent a hydraulic lock and damaging the engine." Red smiled at Jamie. "It's not like your dad's little Cessna."

"I'll say," Jamie replied.

"Okay, we're down to the last step. Remove the electrical heaters." He and Jamie pulled out the heaters from the engine and cockpit, then Red waved them all to get inside. "Climb aboard and find a seat. You can all decide whose riding shotgun."

"Me!" Jamie yelled, then hesitated and turned to his mom. "Is that okay?"

"I guess so. You have the best eyes anyway," said Karen.

Jamie jumped into the front seat next to Red. The women took the two seats directly behind and strapped themselves in.

"Here we go." Red primed and cranked the big engine. The big 600-horsepower engine roared to life then settled to a smooth grumble.

Pattie said something Karen couldn't hear over the engine

"I said it sounds like a Harley Davidson," Pattie yelled.

Red turned around and pointed at headsets hanging next to their seats. Karen saw her son already had his headset on. She and Pattie put on their headsets, adjusted the mike booms, and did their radio checks. "Everyone hear me okay?" Announced red, and they all replied.

"Need to let the oil temp warm up a bit before we move out," Red said. As they waited, she listened to him talking to the tower.

"Lake Hood tower Norseman November 6159 Echo Request clearance to taxi west for a takeoff to the east and departure Northbound."

"Norseman November 6159 Echo Lake Hood tower, Cleared to taxi as requested."

"59 Echo cleared to taxi."

Red increased the engine power and rocked the elevator controls to break the skis loose from the ice. Once freed, the big airplane slid ahead across the frozen lake, bouncing on the rough spots. He scanned his instruments and adjusted them as they slid forward

"Gotta do engine checks on the roll, no brakes on skis," he told Jamie, who nodded back.

When they reached the west end of the lake, Red throttled back and looked around at his passengers. "Everybody strapped in and ready?" When he got thumbs up from each of them, he contacted the tower again.

"Norseman 59 Echo ready for takeoff to the east."

"Norseman, 6159 Echo cleared for takeoff East, Northbound departure approved," the tower replied.

"91 Echo cleared for takeoff"

Red slowly added power. The big engine had barely reached full power as the airplane sped across the ice, and lifted off within seconds.

"Wow. That was quick," Jamie said. "I guess this is a pretty light load for this plane."

"Yep." Red turned them north and leveled out at 9,500 feet, pulling the power back to cruise at 130 knots.

Jamie watched his every move. "Too bad it doesn't have dual controls. I could help you fly."

Old Red chuckled and shook his shaggy grey head.

The sky over Anchorage was clear and cold, a cloud-free uninterrupted blue, but further north towards Mount McKinley were scattered clouds. They flew north following the railroad and Talkeetna, a major town by Alaskan standards, soon came into view.

Red spoke into the mike. "Won't be long now till we make our first turnoff into the mountains."

Red followed the canyons, turning in here, following a frozen stream bed there. Before long, he pulled the power back and lowered the flaps, slowing the airplane. "Keep your eyes peeled around the next bend. We're getting close to my secret lake."

All eyes scanned the terrain for any sign of a downed plane, a signal fire, or anything else that might indicate Jim and Ronnie were down there somewhere. Red rounded the corner and lined up with a snow-covered lake in the distance. "There it is get ready for a landing." He touched the plane down smoothly on the ice, plowing through deep snow, and taxied to the shoreline.

When he shut down the engine, a surreal quiet engulfed them. The sudden lack of noise echoed in their ears in what would have been total silence if not for the crackle and ticks of the engine cooling.

They looked out the windows, but there was nothing to see but the empty snow-covered beach. No plane, no sign of life.

"Let's go take a look around. See if we can spot any evidence they were here," said Red.

The four of them climbed down from the airplane.

"This is where their campsite should have been. I had a big pile of firewood right over there and it's all gone so somebody's been here." Red turned in place, then pointed ahead. "Hey, what's that over there?"

Jamie ran over and tugged at a piece of fabric sticking up through the snow. As the heavy layers of white fell away, a collapsed tent emerged. Karen sucked in a breath, hope and dread colliding inside her.

"Do you recognize it?" Red asked.

"It's Jim's. I was with him when he bought it. But why would they have left it here?"

"I'd guess they got a break in the weather and wanted to get out quick. Now we just have to figure out which way they went. Let's get back in the air. Don't want to waste daylight."

Within minutes they took off again.

Red spoke to them over the headset intercom as the plane lifted and turned. "There's no telling which way they went, which means we got to search in every direction. I'll go low and slow around the radius of the camp, as close to it as I can, that is. There's some high terrain we have to stay clear of, but they would have had to do the same. You need to look for whatever don't seem right. Watch for color. Anything that stands out.

They flew around and around, each completed circle was followed by another, growing ever wider, slowly but steadily expanding the search. The four of them kept their eyes focused on the ground below, straining to see something, anything. Hours went by with nothing but unending shades of white and gray.

"Our fuel's getting low and we're going to lose the sun before long," Red exhaled a long deep breath. "Sorry, Misses, but we need to head back. At least now we know for sure they were here. When we get back, I'll give the FAA the map coordinates for the campsite. That way search-and-rescue will have a positive starting place."

Karen nodded but couldn't speak, her sadness and disappointment were too raw in her throat. She glanced at Pattie who had tears running down her cheeks and looked away before she started to cry as well. Jamie sat silently in the front seat, still staring out his window down at the ground below, not yet ready to admit defeat. No one spoke again for the entire flight back to Lake Hood.

After landing and helping Red secure the plane for the night, they accompanied him to the FAA office and listened as he showed the officer on duty the location of the campsite on a sectional chart. The officer, in turn, passed the information on to Elmendorf Search and Rescue and the civil air patrol.

"They'll be up searching at first light if the weather holds, but I have to warn you, the forecast is for another low-pressure system to move into the area. That means more snow," he told them.

Karen felt like her body was made of lead as she exited the FAA office. Every step took her further away from her missing husband.

Beside her, Jamie walked in silence, head down. Red sighed heavily and patted her son's shoulder.

No, Karen thought, w*e can't give up.* "Red, I appreciate your help."

He shook his head and didn't look at her "It's my fault for sending them out there."

"No, that was Jim's decision, not yours. Or mine. But you know that area better than anyone, so I want us to continue searching. We'll go with you, just like we did today, every day that the weather allows. I'll pay for the gas and your time. Jim and Ronnie are out there somewhere, and we need to find them. Meanwhile, you'll stay with us."

"What?" Red stopped walking and looked up at her. "No. I can't do that, Missy. I'd be taking advantage of your hospitality. Ain't right."

"I insist!" She heard the sharpness in her voice, half-anger half desperation, and took a breath to calm down. "It's not charity. I need you sober, and I don't trust you to stay that way on your own. I want to keep an eye on you."

He scowled and looked away. "Don't think Jimmy'd like it much."

"Well, he's not here. I am. You'll stay in our guest room until I say otherwise." She turned away and headed for his pick-up. She'd take the wheel and make sure he ended up back at her

house. She didn't ask for permission or wait for Red to agree.
There was no need. She'd decided for him.

Chapter 14
Ronnie's Leg

November 4, 1973

Jim woke to the delicious smell of cooked meat. Not knowing where he was at first, he bolted upright trying to orient himself. Ronnie lay on his side next to him facing away, and Elijah was setting out wooden utensils and plates on a table in the kitchen area of the cave. Flickering candles all around cast a warm inviting glow. Jim rubbed his face and took a long breath.

"Hungry?" Elijah asked.

Hungry didn't cut it. "Yeah. Starved. We haven't had much of anything to eat in days."

"Figured as much. Got some grilled moose steaks, beans, and vegetables here. You boys are welcome to come and get it."

"Thanks." Jim reached over and jiggled Ronnie to wake him. "Time to eat."

No response.

"Hey, Ronnie?" Jim pulled on Ronnie's shoulder and rolled him onto his back. Ronnie's eyes stayed closed, his face a paler shade of white than usual, but his cheeks were flushed. Jim laid the back of his hand on Ronnie's forehead, finding it hot with fever. Fearing the worst, he ripped the furs off and looked at the trap-ravaged right leg. The red streaks had crawled up through his thigh. "That poison's still in him. It's working its way up. We've got to do something. He needs penicillin."

"Don't got no penny whatever, but my tea usually does the trick? Lemme take a look." Elijah set down the plates and came over. Looking down at Ronnie's leg, he pursed his lips and scowled. "You're right. It looks bad, really bad. Seeing poison like this, doctors in my day would say the only chance of stopping it is to cut off the leg."

"Christ!" Jim covered his face for a moment to collect himself, then dropped his hands and nodded. "Okay. Okay. Better to lose a leg than a life. We'll need a saw, and plenty of alcohol if you got it."

"I do, but I got a better idea than sawing off this poor boy's leg if you would trust me."

Jim looked up at him. "What idea?"

"I said, you got to trust me, 'cause I ain't willing to show you just yet.

"Show me what?" Jim scowled at him.

Elijah scowled back. "You don't listen too well, do ya? Now are you gonna trust me, or not? If not, I'll go get you that saw, and you can take your friend outside to butcher him. I don't want to hear him screaming and have him bleeding all over my floor."

"You won't help me do it?"

Elijah shook his head. "No, I won't. Seen enough of that to last me a lifetime and then some."

"But he'll die if we don't."

"Might anyway even if you do. Most men can't handle the shock and even cuttin off the limb you can't be sure of stoppin' all the bad blood. Better you should trust me."

The thought of sawing off Ronnie's leg horrified Jim. Doing it alone without Elijah's help felt insurmountable. But to just walk away and let this man whom he didn't know take over with some unexplained cure sounded like a death sentence. "I don't know. I'm sure you mean well, but—"

"Son, when I came here, I was near to death myself. This place saved me then and I believe it can save your friend now. If'n you're willing to trust me."

Jim looked down at Ronnie and continued to hesitate. Neither option was good.

"Unless you were looking forward to sawin' off his leg."

"No! God, no!" His stomach knotted at the prospect. "Okay, fine, go ahead. Do whatever it is you have in mind."

"Good choice." Elijah walked away and opened the door of the cave to the outside. He gave a long loud whistle, then stood back and waited. A minute later, the huge grizzly bear they'd seen before squeezed through the door and lumbered inside.

"What the hell?" Jim scrambled back to stand behind Elijah. "Why did you call him in here?"

"Insurance. I appreciate that you've decided to trust me, but the sentiment aint exactly mutual just yet. He'll make sure you keep your word." Elijah picked Ronnie up in his arms. "Wait here, till I get back. Try to follow me, and Grizzy won't like it." Elijah exited into a side tunnel and the bear sat down blocking the way and fixing its brown predatory eyes on Jim. Jim stood still, staring back. At least the bear seemed calm at the moment, but he didn't want to make any sudden moves that could alarm him. For a long time, Jim remained standing, unmoving, but he observed him scratch lazily and lift his black nose to sniff at the food-laden air. Both Jim and the bear looked over at the platter of grilled moose steaks.

"Help yourself," Jim said and slowly gestured at the table.

The bear grunted in response, licked his chops, and wriggled his black nose. Jim hoped the bear would go for the food so he could slip away, but the bear stayed where he was. The bear's determination to guard Jim took precedence over his stomach. Jim respected that even if he didn't like it. Maybe this was an opportunity to make friends.

"You want me to get you one?" Jim asked.

The bear grunted again and surprised Jim by bobbing his head up and down with enthusiasm. The answer seemed clear enough. "Okay." Jim took a cautious step toward the table. The bear rose to all fours to watch but made no move from his assigned post. Jim reached for one of the steaks thinking he was about to befriend a grizzly bear or get killed by one. He lifted the juicy steak in the air and dangled it, its juice dripping onto the floor. The bear opened his jaws wide in anticipation as if expecting Jim to step forward and drop the meat into his gaping mouth. There was no way he was getting that close. Instead, he flung the steak so it landed a foot in front of the bear's forepaws.

The bear looked at the meat lying on the dusty floor in front of him, then snorted in disgust and turned his head aside.

"Really! You won't eat it because it's on the floor? What kind of bear are you anyway?"

Grizzy licked his jaws, then sat back down in front of the side tunnel, leaving the thrown steak untouched. He stared at Jim and cocked his big head, waiting.

Jim twisted his mouth, reassessing the situation. This was not an ordinary bear, but one worth befriending. Still, he wasn't about to trust it enough to risk losing a hand or an arm trying to deliver a steak into its mouth. He picked up another slab of the cooked meat and laid it on a plate, then set the plate on the floor. He slid the plate toward the bear with an extended foot then backed away. "There. All nice and clean."

The bear shuffled forward and scarfed up the steak. Then he nosed the empty plate across the floor back to Jim. The bear looked up, waiting.

"I take it you want seconds," Jim said. The bear bobbed his head again, so Jim refilled the plate, set it on the floor, and sent it sliding back. Again it was scarfed up in an instant and the plate returned. Jim set the last steak on the plate and slid it back. The bear gobbled up the meat.

"You know that's my dinner you're eating, right?"

The bear froze in the middle of chewing then spat what was left of the mangled steak in his mouth back onto the plate and put his nose down ready to slide it back toward Jim.

"No, no, that's okay. I'm just going to have vegetables. I want you to have it."

The bear lifted his head to look at Jim then seemed to come to a decision. He snatched up the half-chewed steak in his teeth and swallowed it down.

Am I really having a conversation with a bear?

"Oh good, you're still alive," Elijah said as he came through the tunnel and walked forward to stand next to the bear. "Glad to see the two of you getting along."

"Where's Ronnie? What did you do with him?" Jim asked in alarm.

"Getting the cure takes time. We have to leave him to it and hope for the best. Don't you worry none, I'll be checking on him regular like." Elijah's gaze went to the table and empty platter where the steaks had been. "Figured you was hungry but didn't expect you to eat up all them steaks by your lonesome."

"I had help." Jim gestured at the bear, which promptly let out a long rolling belch.

"Grizzy. Shame on you," Elijah said, shaking his head. "You know cooked meat upsets your stomach. Better get on outa here before you stink up the place."

Grizzy replied with another belch and went out the door. Elijah waved a hand in the air and shut the door behind him. It was then that Ely noticed the soiled steak on the ground and picked it up. "I should have warned you not to feed him. He loves grilled moose, but it sure don't love him."

"Sorry," Jim replied.

"No matter. He'll be fine. And we'll do just fine with what's left. I'll wash this one off and give it another minute on the grill to heat it up. Then let's sit down and eat."

Jim watched Elijah wash the dirt off the steak in the bucket then followed him outside, where a fire burned inside a homemade oven with a metal grill on top. A few minutes later, the steak was steaming hot again making Jim's empty stomach growl and his mouth water.

"You've got quite a setup here," Jim commented.

"We make do."

"We?"

"Grizzy and me." Elijah scooped up the steak and went back into the cave with Jim at his heels. Elijah gestured for Jim to sit down as he dropped into a chair and scooped food onto a plate. Jim followed his example. He was ravenous, made even more so by watching the bear eat those steaks, so much so that he forgot to worry about Ronnie as he tried to satisfy the empty pit in his stomach. He kept shoveling and swallowing until he filled up at last and then the worry about Ronnie returned.

Elijah finished eating long before Jim but sat waiting.

"Thanks," Jim said, wiping his mouth. "Can we talk about Ronnie and this cure of yours? I'd like to see him, see how he's doing."

"What the hell are you doin in my valley?" Elijah asked in a deadly calm voice that took Jim back. Elijah wore a mean look and his fists balled up. "Nobody's gotten down that mountain alive in all the years I been here. No one ever, 'cept me, but somehow you did. Now start talkin, and it better be the truth, 'cause I get real mean when lied to."

"I already told you it was unintentional. Coming here was a pure accident." Jim explained again what happened to them, but this time in more detail about the unexpected weather, their plane crash, climbing down the mountain, and then seeing the trail leading down into the forest where he'd found them. Elijah listened wearing an intense scowl on his face.

"Just a plane crash, huh? Never understood why a man would want to trust his life to some flying contraption that can fall out of the sky whenever it chooses." His scowl finally softened, and he chuckled. "And you spent the night in a tree well? Well, I gotta give you boys credit for staying alive. More than I can say about anyone else who's comin' this way. Those mountains are littered with men's bones. If it turns out you're lyin I'll have your hide decoratin the floor, but I'm choosin to believe ya for now. Don't make me regret it."

"I won't, so long as Ronnie is okay. If he's not, then you and I have a problem."

Elijah grinned at him. "Warms my heart, that kind of loyalty considerin the fact that havin a problem with me means havin a problem with Grizzy."

Jim–nodded and smiled. "Yeah, I figured that out. Look, Elijah. I don't want to get into a pissing match with you, let alone with that pet bear of yours, but my friend is ill and you ran off with him with no explanation. I'm worried about him."

Ely sighed and nodded. "He should be fine, but like I said, it'll take a little time."

"How long?"

Elijah shrugged. "A day, maybe two, hard to say. I'll keep a close eye on him and bring him back here when he's ready."

Jim didn't like all this secrecy. "I don't understand why I can't see him."

"No, you don't, and I'm not ready to explain it."

"You said you believed me."

Ely smiled. "Believin's one thing, trustin's another."

Chapter 15
Elijah's story

November 4, 1973

Jim rubbed his forehead in frustration. He couldn't afford to alienate Elijah, let alone the bear. "Okay, I get it. You don't know us and trust takes time. Maybe if I trust you, you'll start doing the same."

"Maybe. Once I figure out why you're here."

Jim shook his head and sighed. Didn't he just finish telling Elijah the whole story? What was this guy's problem? "If this place is as hard to find as you say, how did you get here?"

"Well, now, that's a long story, but seein as we got all the time in the world, reckon I best start at the beginnin." Elijah leaned back and propped his feet up on another chair, getting comfortable. " You can call me Eli, sounds less formal. Anyway, I spent my boyhood in Virginia. Didn't like it much there and ran away to join the army, then came west after the war."

Jim thought Eli looked to be in his mid-to-late forties, too old for Vietnam, too young for World War II. He guessed the one in between. "You mean the Korean War?"

"I ain't never heard of any war by that name. We called it the War Between the States. Some folks called it the Civil War."

Jim raised his eyebrows. *Oh, crap. This guy is wacko.* He kept that conclusion to himself and neutralized his expression so as not to telegraph his dismay. As Eli continued his tale, Jim listened and observed in controlled silence.

"At thirteen, I was too young to fight so they said I could either be a bugle boy or I could work in the ammunition factory making Mollie balls and gunpowder for the army. Blowin a Horn didn't have much appeal and I thought maybe I'd learn some kind of valuable skill doin ammunition so that's what I chose. I worked doing that till I turned 15, and could pass for 18. Army took me then, gave me a rifle, and sent me to the front lines. Still got my old trusty Springfield."

Jim looked over at the collector item hanging on the wall, the same flintlock rifle Eli had aimed at his face. It looked well-used but also well-maintained.

"Some of the men reworked their rifles to percussion but I never trusted that. Anyways, when the war ended, I headed back home and found the old house I lived in was gone, burned to the ground, and most of my people was killed by Yankees."

Jim knew from his school days that the Civil War ended in 1865, a hundred and eleven years ago. He didn't believe a word of this but listened without comment.

"So being a young man with no ties, I went west like everybody else, workin my way through the territories. Took a job doin hard labor in the fields of Kansas for a while. Learned to ride and went west again movin' cattle. Ended up on a ranch in the Dakotas where I did some Indian fighting when there weren't no negotiating with 'em. Helped knowin their ways, seein as I was one of em."

"You're an Indian?"

"Half. My mother was Iroquois."

"Looks like we have something in common. My mother was Inuit."

Ely narrowed his eyes at Jim, looking closer. "Maybe that explains it."

"Explains what?"

"Why you're here."

Jim didn't know what to say to that. "Didn't mean to interrupt. You were telling me how you got here."

"So I was. Some years later, I heard bout a gold rush up here in Alaska. Sounded like a man could make his fortune here, so my son and I traveled up to the Yukon."

"You were married by then?"

"I was. Mayella was a fine-looking woman, sweet as molasses and even sweeter on me. Didn't appreciate it then but she was my real treasure. Our son, Russell was a good strong healthy boy and eager to make his fortune. We found gold prospecting around Dawson Creek, but not much. Then there was a big strike in Nome, so we went up there. Never found no gold, but we got jobs in the camp. It was a regular income and I was tired of prospectin, so I figured I'd settle down there and send for my wife. Russell kept on chasin the gold, goin from Nome to the beaches near Fort Davis and then on to Fairbanks. Mayella and I joined him in Fairbanks and I got me a job in a lumber mill."

"How old were you then?"

"Let's see now. It would have been around 1905 or so, that would make me around fifty-seven, I guess. Speaking of planes, that's where I saw my first one. It was the day before the 4th of July."

"1913," Jim said. That was a date in Alaskan history he knew. Two Fairbanks businessmen hired an aviator inventor, James V. Martin, to come to Alaska for an exhibition. Martin brought the plane to Fairbanks by boat and train, assembled it there, and flew it over an amazed crowd of people who didn't think flight even possible.

"Quite a sight," Eli continued. "Could hardly believe it. Anyway, right after that, Russell went to work on the railroad they was building, and we all moved on to Talkeetna. I was too old by then for them to hire me, so I spent my days building a cabin, a good one. When Russell found himself a woman in town to marry and started a family of his own, I helped him build another cabin for them nearby. We was all doing real good till the sickness came.

It swept through the town like a bad wind, and nobody could stop it. My boy's boy went first, then his wife, and then him. They had the TB. Mayella tended to 'em all, God bless her. I buried the four of em out behind our cabin. I remember carving the dates into their crosses. April, May, and June 1926. Couldn't stay there no more with all of them gone, and I was startin to feel kind of sickly myself. Figured the end was comin for me, too. Nobody was left to sit by my bedside, and I wouldn't have wanted them to anyway. I decided to go off and live the rest of my days where I wouldn't bother no one and no one would bother me. Got me a burro, loaded it up, and took off into the mountains. I was gonna live off the land for as long as I could, then just lie down somewhere's peaceful-like and let the good Lord take me." Ely lapsed into silence then, a distant look of sad contemplation shadowed his features.

"Quite a story," said Jim, but he was doing the math in his head, none of which was adding up. "So um, you must have been pretty old by then, right?"

"Well, now, leme figure." Eli rolled his eyes to the ceiling and scratched his chin. "I reckon I was around 78 that summer I went walkin into the mountains. Didn't know where I was a goin and I was gettin sicker by the day, but it was like somethin' was callin' to me so I just kept on walkin. I was gettin weaker, wrackin coughin fits, hard to breathe, spitting up blood, pukin, but kept walkin deeper and deeper into these mountains, not knowin where or why, just that I had to keep goin. Each day grew colder, less game, and snow started fallin. I was losin weight. The grass was long gone, and my burro died. I ate him though he was pretty much wasted away.

Jim listened, transfixed, seeing the story unfold in his mind.

"That last day, I was in a blinding whiteout, near frozen to the bone. My clothes weren't meant for such a bitter cold. In the distance, I heard a bear bellowin. I thought it was a sign. Decided either that bear was goin to eat me or I was goin to eat it. I followed the sound till I saw the bear. A big sow, her teats heavy with milk, with a beautiful thick coat, but she was limping, hurt bad. I wanted her, needed her—for food, for warmth. I was almost dead and she was life. She moved ahead into the blindin snowstorm and I stumbled after her. When I fell behind, she slowed as if waiting for me. I kept following, sometimes seeing her, other times just her tracks. She kept waiting for me, looking back at me, and then suddenly she just seemed to disappear into the mountain. I didn't know it then, but she was leading me here, through that hidden entrance you came through. I followed her between the giant boulders at the cliff face then on through the maze into this small canyon. Gettin closer, I could smell her heat and see blood marking the way in. I followed the trail through the cliff, and on through to the end of this canyon right up to the sheer cliff face. I swore there was no way that she-bear was getting away from me. We were goin to have it out one way or the other. Turned out she had no intention of gettin away.

"She was waiting for me in front of the cliff face out there. With her last bit of strength, she stood up on her hind legs and roared at me. I thought she was getting ready to attack so I brought up my rifle and fired true, bringin her down. When I got close, I saw that she was already injured so bad in her chest and belly that she would have died even without the help of my bullet.

"Just a few yards away was the entrance to this cave. That she-bear saved me, gave me life with her flesh, her fur, and her cave in this magical canyon. This was her home and had been for a long time. It was like she knew it was her time and wanted someone to take over.

"In the dark, I could only see a short way inside this cave. It smelled of bear, and there was lots of bones and fur around. I was exhausted, and could hardly stand up, so I laid down in the corner right over there and closed my eyes, but it wasn't long afore I woke with a start, feeling something warm and fuzzy cuddled up beside me. Scared me near to death, but turned out it was just a tiny bear cub, weak and hungry, still needing its mother's milk. Felt like I owed that she-bear for leading me here so I carried the little cub out to its mother to nurse what milk it could. She was still warm so I knew it would be okay. Then I skinned and dressed her for myself. I needed her fur coat for warmth and her flesh for food. From that day on I took care of her valley. Fixed up this cave and made it my home. Took care of her cub, feeding him her milk first, then mashed up fish and berries, until he grew big and strong enough to fend for himself."

"And that's him."

Eli nodded. "Named him Grizzy. He's a good bear, smart too."

"How did you manage to do all that? You said you were sick."

"I was, but as the days passed, I felt better, stronger, like some new energy was flowin through me. I didn't know what was happenin to me but it felt good. Didn't have nothin to go back to, so I stayed and haven't seen another human face since. Til now."

Chapter 16
Ronnie's recovery

November 7, 1973

Eli was quite the woodworker. He made Ronnie a proper leg splint and a matching beautifully carved crutch, with fur covering the top and leather-wrapped handhold. "This should help him get around when he's ready."

"Beautiful work," Jim replied. He'd been careful not to offend Eli during Ronnie's absence these last few days lest he sic his pet grizzly bear on him. He hid his worry and pretended to trust Eli completely. Gradually Eli lowered his guard, turning more talkative as time went by. Meanwhile, Jim drank Eli's herbal tea, which kept him relatively pain-free despite his bruised ribs, and waited for his strength to return in full.

"Can I ask you a question?" Jim ventured on the third day of Ronnie's absence.

"Sure," said Eli.

"I was pretty banged up when we got here and think maybe I heard you wrong. I thought you said fought in the Civil War or did I hear you wrong?"

"No. You heard me right. I saw my first battle when I was a boy of fifteen. That's what I was referring to when I said I'd seen enough of men's legs bein' sawed off for a lifetime."

"Okay, sorry I may sound a little confused, but I'm pretty sure that war started in 1861 and ended in 1865, which means you would have been born around what…1849, 50?"

"Hmmm…lemme see now." Eli pondered a minute, stroking his beard. "Close as I can recollect, I was 13 when I tried to join up. I ran off after the war began." His fingers twitched in the air as if counting, "So guess that'd make my birthing around 1848."

"1848? Are you sure?"

"I could be off a year, but no more'n that. I remember for certain they wouldn't let me have a rifle afore I turned fifteen, and that was a couple of years later. Spent the first two in a gunpowder factory.

"A man never forgets his first taste of war— seein' what a bloody awful mess it is. Our side won that skirmish, though it was hard to tell with all the carnage. A year later, the war ended, and I went west."

"This is 1973. If the war ended in 1865." Jim did the math in his head, "That would make you l25 years old now."

"I know how old I am, and I know what year it is. I even know the date. I keep track." He pointed to the far wall of the cave, where small notches were cut into the stone,

Jim walked over to take a closer look at the wall. He'd noticed the markings on the wall before but hadn't recognized their significance until now. A long series of half-inch cuts started in groups of seven, then evolved into squared blocks setting out an entire calendar year. He counted fourteen blocks. The first read 1928, with an additional three years listed for each. The years listed went up to 1973. This was a handmade calendar and he had to admit it seemed to corroborate Eli's story, but things still didn't add up. The man standing a few feet away from him looked to be in his mid-forties, maybe fifty years old at most, and that was stretching it.

"By my reckoning, I'm a hundred and twenty-five years old now. Lived longer than most, I suppose," Eli said and let out a long sigh. "Not sure why this place picked me. Can't be nothing to do with me deserving it. I'm wonderin' if the same can be said for you."

"You think it picked you? This place?"

"Ain't no other explanation for it. This valley here is strange, like it's alive, and knows you. Could be magical or something else. I don't know how it works and don't expect I ever will. I just know what it does."

"And what exactly is that?"

"Keeps you alive."

"That's the cure you were talking about?"

Eli nodded. "It's this canyon, this cave, the water, all of it."

"Then why did you have to take Ronnie somewhere else?"

"There are certain places here where the cure's more concentrated. Works faster. I figured your friend needed that."

"Would you please take me to him? Let me see him. I won't stop worrying until I do. Whatever you're worried about, you don't need to be. You've saved our lives. We owe you."

"Yeah, you do." Eli studied him for a long while. "Ah well. Who am I to question this place? T'warn't me who invited you and Grizzy didn't kill you when you showed up, so I suppose you're meant to be here. Alright, then, come on. I'll show ya where he is."

Eli led him to the adjoining tunnel that opened into another cave, narrow at the entrance and then widening into a slightly larger cavern lit with an ethereal blue. Stalactites hung like icicles from the ceiling mirrored by icy white formations growing upward from the floor to meet them. The only sound was a gentle trickling of water running down the glistening walls. His eyes widened with wonder taking it all in. "Where the heck is that blue light coming from?"

"Glow worms," Eli explained, pointing upward. "They like the moisture in here. Light up the whole place."

Jim followed his gesture and saw what looked like thousands upon thousands of blue stars covering the entire cavern's lofty ceiling. Most of the stars stayed put, but a few flit across the dark background like comets. "Wow! They're alive?"

"These are like the kind I remember seeing as a boy in Virginia, but never so many like this. They're just worms, but they got blue "lanterns" on each end. Impressive, ain't it?"

"Yeah. Amazing," said Jim momentarily stunned. Then he remembered why he was here. "So where's Ronnie?"

"Not far. We'll need to make our light from here…gets real dark, but what's ahead's good for whatever ails ya, I guarantee. Come on." He led Jim down a tunnel, lighting candles along the way.

"You sure have a lot of candles," Jim commented.

"Make 'em from animal fat and rawhide. Lemon juice makes em smell good."

Around the next corner, the tunnel opened into an even larger cavern of fantastic natural beauty. Massive stalactites stabbed down from the ceiling, and giant stalagmites stood guard like huge carved ivory statues. Ahead Jim saw steaming hot pools that glowed like turquoise-colored jewels. Jim stared in awe, speechless.

"There's your friend," Eli pointed ahead. "Let's see how he's doing."

Jim gasped seeing a shadowy form lying suspended in one of the pools surrounded by lit candles. He knew vernal hot springs could change from comfortably warm to scalding in seconds. He feared the worst and ran forward. "Ronnie!"

Eli shook his head with evident disapproval.

Jim felt Ronnie's neck for a pulse, relieved to find one. "Hey, wake up." He tapped Ronnie's face lightly at first then with more force until Ronnie sputtered and opened his eyes.

"What the...? Why are you hitting me, dude?"

Jim exhaled a deep breath. "Are you okay?"

"I was till you started slapping me." Ronnie noticed Eli standing behind Jim and smiled. "Hey, Eli, thanks for the snacks earlier."

"Snacks? This whole time you've been hanging out in a hot tub binging on snacks?"

"Don't get yourself in a knot. I've still got some food left if you want some."

Jim shook his head and got to his feet. "How long were you going to stay down here, letting me wonder if you were still alive?"

"Hey, I'm injured here, remember? Not like I had a choice. And I figured Eli was keeping you informed."

"Course I was. I let him know I was taking good care of you, that you were healin' up fine and not to worry."

"But you wouldn't tell me where he was. You had that bear of yours keeping an eye on me, keeping me away."

"Whoa. Wondered why you didn't come to see me." Ronnie scowled in Eli's direction. "What's the deal, man? Why would you do that?"

"You needed time to heal. I was concerned your friend here wouldn't understand and would try to drag you out of there."

"Maybe if you tried explaining things instead of keeping secrets—"

"Why should I? Don't owe you nothin.... least of all my trust."

Jim took a moment to stop himself from making an angry retort and cautioned himself from making matters worse. He slowly nodded. "You're right. You don't know me. I'm grateful for the help you've given us. Even more grateful for what you've done for Ronnie. I was scared for him, that's all."

Eli still regarded him with a skeptical look.

"Thanks, man. But I'm cool. See." Ronnie swung both feet up on the edge of the pool so that his legs were exposed. In the dim light, Jim squatted closer to see. Although Ronnie's legs were flushed pink from the pool's heat, the angry red streaks were gone.

Eli poked at Ronnie's legs. "Don't see any sign of infection anymore. Think it might be time to start exercising a bit now.

"Oh hell, yeah. Give me a hand, dude." Ronnie plunged his feet back into the glowing pool and reached out an arm to Jim.

Jim helped him climb out of the pool and sit on the edge. Ely fitted the new splint on the broken leg and handed Ronnie the hand-carved crutch.

"Wow, dude, beautiful woodcarving. Thanks." With their help, Ronnie hoisted himself up and took a tentative step using the crutch. "This feels great. Fits me just right." He took a few more steps and laughed. "Wow. There's no pain in the bear trap leg at all now just a slight twinge where I broke the other one. That magic hot pool worked."

"Magic?" Jim dipped his hand in the water and sniffed the sulfur odor he expected. Just a hot pool, although he couldn't explain the greenish-blue glow.

Ronnie walked around, laughing, then did a little jig. "Look at me, I'm cured."

"That's great. Now, would you mind putting on some clothes?" Jim said.

"Man, you are one uptight dude," Ronnie replied but gathered up a set of neatly folded clothes from a nearby rock and started dressing.

Chapter 17
The tour of the caverns

November 8, 1973

"Hey, Eli how about that tour you promised," Ronnie said. "I've been dying to see it."

"See what?" Jim asked.

"Not sure," Ronnie replied with an enigmatic grin. "But Ely says it makes all this seem like nothing."

"Aye, it's maybe the best or worst thing about this place, certainly the most mind-boggling. You'll hardly believe it even when looking at it with your own eyes. Come on, I'll just have to show you." Eli waived for them to follow. He gave them lit candles and led them deeper into the dark cave and on through more dark tunnels that lead downward. They wound down and down, treading on deeply worn steps at the steepest points that had been carved into the rock. The tunnel looked like a volcanic lava tube that had been carved out in places to widen it. When the last tunnel finally bottomed out, Jim swore he saw light ahead, which made no sense whatsoever. They had to be hundreds of feet below the surface.

The tunnel opened into a massive cave, maybe a mile wide, that was lit up with a bluish light. In front of them was a sandy white beach and beyond that lay a body of blue water extending farther than they could see. Ronnie and Jim froze at the sight, struck dumb with awe. The water had an eerie phosphorous blue glow and seemed to go on and on until disappearing in a distant blue haze

"How do you like my lake?" Eli asked.

"This isn't a lake, it's a freaking ocean!" Jim exclaimed. The underground wonder was overwhelmingly huge and fully lit. He could see the interior of the entire cave and the water stretching on and on as if they were outdoors on an overcast morning, but there was a solid roof of ice above them, maybe a hundred feet high. Ely was right, Jim didn't believe his eyes.

"Pretty amazing ain't it? Don't know what's on the other side, or how far it goes?

About twenty years ago I got really curious about what was on the other side so I started building a raft. Hauled that stack of logs over there down from above and started buildin. Then one day I saw this thing out there stick its big head out of the water as it went by. I don't have no idea what it was but it was really big. I decided right then and there. That was the end of my raft buildin' I weren't never goin' out on that water."

"How big was that thing? Any idea what it was?" Jim asked.

"I reckon the head and neck were bout as tall as you. The rest of it was underwater but rippled back about as long as two or three boats. It's really big. Got no idea what it is though. I've seen it a bunch of times over the years since then, not all of it just like a big shadow. Ripples the surface, kind of splashes a bit, then it's gone. Almost like it's bashful, afraid to show itself."

That wood pile over there is as far as I got with my raft. I ain't touched it in twenty years."

Jim stared at the blue lake, overwhelmed by its very existence, wondering what secrets it held and where it might lead.

"Look at those wall paintings over there. Lots of animal pictures, some I recognize but lots of pictures don't make much sense. That wall is probably fifty feet high with pictures all the way up. Seen nothin' like it before." Said Eli.

"I got more to show you," Eli said, pointing across the sand to what looked like an orchard. "You saw my lemon trees up above, right? Ever see citrus growing anywhere in Alaska before?"

Both men shook their heads. "Not till we came here."

"You think that was amazing, wait until you see what I've got growing down here. Come on, take a look."

The three men headed across the beach that seemed to sparkle with golden flakes, Ronnie hobbling on his crutch, toward a grove of trees, flanked with long neat rows of green plants. As they got closer, it seemed as if the plants got larger and larger. Jim found himself staring at what looked like a blue-tinged cauliflower bigger than all of their three heads put together.

"These are the same fruits and vegetables growin' up in the valley but down here, they turn out a little different. What do you think?"

Jim gaped at the flourishing oversized garden, more robust than anything he'd ever seen in a greenhouse. The orchard contained a variety of fruit trees— peaches, apples, and lemons— and not a chewed leaf to be seen. The fruits and vegetables were all much larger than normal, and all of them were oddly tinged with blue.

"Never seen anything like it," said Jim.

"Wow, dude, this is incredible! You must have one of the greenest thumbs ever," said Ronnie, shaking his head. "I bet you could grow some amazing trophy weed."

"No weeds down here. No pests of any sort. This is the easiest farmin I ever done. Just plant a seed and let it grow. When I left Talkeetna, I was plannin' on settlin' down somewhere, buildin' me a cabin, and livin' off the land till the TB finally took me. Along with my sack of grub, I brung some seeds to plant come summer. I had a sack of lemons with me, too, cause they keep well and are good to flavor game. When I found this lake, I'd spend hours just sittin' down here starin' at it. I brung food along and buried the leftovers.

"Never thought nothin would come of it, but next thing I know, little green shoots were sproutin' up all over the place. Afore long I had a little grove of lemon trees. I figured if lemons could grow, so could other seeds so I started planting them down here, and damned if every single one of 'em didn't' come up. You wouldn't believe how fast. I grew up farmin and I knew it just weren't right, so I decided it had to be a blessing. Being the God-fearing man I was, I thought I'd stumbled on God's special green acre itself – the lost Garden of Eden. I prayed a lot in those early days, askin' why I'd been brought here, prayin for guidance, lookin' for answers." Eli sighed and fell silent.

"Did you find any?" Ronnie asked.

Eli shrugged. "No. Not really. No God either, far as I can tell, 'cept for the Mountain maybe, but that could be just my imagination. I been livin' alone for a long time now. Grizzy's good company but not much for conversation. A man's mind starts to question what's real and what ain't when left to itself for too long. That's why I've brought you down here. I need to know if what I'm seeing is as real to you as it is to me."

"It certainly feels real, but…," Jim turned in a slow circle and stared about, "I can't begin to explain it."

"Either of you ever dropped acid?" Ronnie asked. "Feels kind of like this. What exactly is in that tea you keep giving us?"

"I don't know what acid you speak of, but the tea's ingredients are just water, lemons, and herbs from this garden," Eli replied.

Jim bent down to examine a blue-tinged leaf. "I suppose it could have some hallucinogenic properties, but even so why would we all be dreaming the same thing?"

Ronni shrugged. "Power of suggestion, group hypnosis?" He and Jim both looked at Eli.

"I ain't no medicine man and it's not the tea," Ely said. "I've experimented, cut things out of my diet one by one, went without the tea for months. This place always stays the same. If you boys are seein what I'm seein, it means it's real. I'm not drugged, and I'm not crazy. Never really thought I was, but now that you boys are here, I know it for sure."

Ronnie and Jim wore half-smiles of disbelief, shaking their heads and looking around at the grove of blue-tinged trees. The oversized vegetables and herbs exhibited the same strange hue. Beyond the sandy white beach, the endless water glowed as if lit up with magical blue fireflies. The lit underground lake was stunning to behold, but incongruous, and unfathomable, especially because they were viewing it deep below the surface.

"Where's all this light coming from?" Jim asked.

"The blue water reflects off the ice above us like a mirror," Eli said. "Lights up the whole place."

"Yeah, I can see that. But why does the water glow like that?"

Eli shrugged. "Was kinda hoping you could tell me."

"Must be some sort of bioluminescence," Ronnie said. "I've seen it in the ocean at night sometimes, but never as bright as this. Not even close."

Jim stared at the endless blue-lit water for a long time, lost for words. Finally, he tore his gaze away. "So, you say nothing was growing down here before you planted the seeds you brought with you?" Jim asked, trying to ground himself in something concrete. "And every seed sprouted?"

"Yep. Every single one. My garden looks mighty healthy, don't it?"

"I'll say," Jim agreed. "So how often do you have to replant?"

"Never. I guess I didn't make myself clear. Nothin' dies here. Not even me."

Chapter 18
Exploring outside

November 12

In the days after seeing the giant underground lake, Jim tried without much success to reconcile both its existence and Eli's with his expectations of reality. He couldn't shake how much this all reminded him of the fantastical Inuit legends his mother had told him when he was a boy. To distract himself from the illogic of everything he'd seen here, he concentrated on Ronnie's recovery. To his relief, Ronnie was doing better, experiencing little pain in his leg now and growing stronger with each passing day. So much so, that Jim started thinking they might soon be able to travel again. He wanted to get out of here and back home where things made sense, the sooner the better.

One evening after sharing a meal of stewed meat and vegetables, the three of them sat at Eli's self-crafted wood dining table drinking Eli's homemade herbal tea. The cave was pleasantly warm from the radiating hot springs below and Eli's huge grizzly bear lay splayed out on the floor like a rug. Jim might have seen it as a peaceful tableau, if not for the fact that the rug was alive.

Jim watched Ronnie fiddling with his camera settings before setting it on the table and aiming the lens at the snoring grizzly lying on the floor.

"The trick to taking photos at night is to open up the lens and make sure nothing moves," Ronnie said. "Did the same thing for those northern lights. I can't wait to develop the film and see how these all come out."

"We need to get home. Our wives must be frantic by now," Jim said.

Ronnie turned to look at him. "Yeah, I know, but I'm kind of stuck here till my leg heals, in case you hadn't noticed."

"Ain't nobody goin nowhere' till breakup anyways," Eli said. "Not till the river outside starts flowin again—gotta be frozen up solid by now."

"I figured as much, but I'm thinking we could build a sled and pull it downriver on the ice," Jim said.

Eli shook his head. "You could, but it'd be suicide."

Silence fell leaving only the sound of the crackling fire.

Eli took a long breath before speaking again. "My first year here, I thought same as you and tried leavin' here in mid-winter to do some trading. Built a sled to haul my furs to the nearest town and load up on supplies. I weren't no fool, so I waited till the weather was lookin good with clear skies. Started makin my way down the river thinkin I ought to reach Talkeetna in two or three weeks, no more. Then it all went to hell. Clouds moved in, the wind picked up, started snowin like it'd never stop, and froze me in place for three, maybe four weeks, trapped on the river in freezin' cold, blowin snow and ice heaves. I started gettin' weak again, coughing my lungs out like the TB was back. If it hadn't been for Grizzy, I'd have been dead for sure."

Hearing his name, the bear opened his eyes and grunted.

"I was barely alive when he found me, but I managed to climb onto his back and he carried me all the way to his home, our home. Once back, the illness went away again and I recovered. Ain't never tried leavin' for any length of time since. Especially not in winter. Figured if the cold didn't get me, the TB would. Now you boys weren't ailing when you arrived, 'cept for that broken leg and some cuts and bruises, so you ought to be able to leave the valley without fallin ill like I did. But not until spring. It's a sure bet, you'd never make it out alive now."

"Spring? You're talking months from now," Ronnie said and leaned back. "Wow that sucks."

Jim scowled at Eli, wondering if he was exaggerating the risk. "We'll keep an eye on the weather… come up with a plan."

Eli chuckled. "Sure. You do that."

"I will. Bet on it. In fact, I'll start by taking a walk out of this canyon tomorrow and see exactly what we're up against. Maybe it's not as bad out there as you think."

"Do as you will," replied Eli. "Some folks just gotta see things for themselves."

The next morning, while Ronnie stayed behind with his still-healing leg, Jim prepared to take that walk outside the valley. He stuck a pair of snowshoes in a back carrier along with his parka, gloves, and hat, and grabbed a walking stick to test snow depth. Eli accompanied him to the end of the valley with the bear trailing behind. When they reached the cleft in the canyon wall that exited to the outer world, Eli stopped and shook Jim's hand.

"Here's where we part ways. Remember what I told you for finding your way out and back again?"

Jim nodded. "Leaving—two rights, a left, another right, then take every left until it opens out. Returning, do it all in reverse."

"Good. Stay close to the opening and mark it well. If you lose sight of it, it can be mighty tough to find again... especially in bad weather."

"I understand. I'm not planning on going far and I know how to mark a trail. I just want to check things out. I'll be back soon." In preparation for colder weather, despite being plenty warm right now, Jim donned his parka, hat, and gloves and then entered the cleft. He wove his way through the maze following Eli's directions until he came to the end and slid out into a world vastly different from the one he'd just left. A blast of freezing air and blowing snow assaulted him, stinging his face and making him gasp at the sudden shock of it. Still standing on the stone ledge of the cliff, he lifted an arm to protect his face and plunged his walking stick out before him and down into a waist-deep powder. *Good thing I brought the snowshoes*, he thought.

A cluster of pine trees stood fifty feet ahead. He remembered those trees from before, but now they looked half as tall with their lower halves buried in white. He also remembered that just beyond those trees lay a long slope opening into a wide expanse. A view from there should give him a clearer understanding of what challenges might lie ahead when attempting to return home. He slipped the snow shoes onto his boots to keep from sinking into the powdery snow. They would also leave a clear trail to follow back to this opening in the rock wall. He stepped down gingerly onto the snow and once he felt his footing secure, worked his way over to the trees. He glanced behind to make sure he could see his trail back to where he had exited the opening in the cliff.

Clear as day, he thought to himself. *I don't know what Eli was so worried about.*

A gust swirled up around him and blew him half a step back, but he leaned into it and pushed ahead, determined to get a look at what lay beyond the trees. He worked his way carefully through the grove of pine trees, giving their trunks a wide berth, where hidden tree wells might lie to trap the unwary. A misstep would send him on a downward ride into a gap between a tree trunk and fallen snow. Getting out again was nearly impossible without help. Once past the trees, he soon reached the edge of the slope overlooking a wide expanse. Peering down he saw deeply buried trees poking up through a vast blanket of white. Not a boulder to be seen anywhere. For a moment he imagined sledding down that smooth white slope. It seemed to go on for miles. What a ride that would be. He felt a growing excitement at the prospect of leaving this mountainous terrain behind so easily. As he stared downward, the view blurred in the distance and he squinted and rubbed his eyes, thinking they were watering in the icy air. He blinked repeatedly trying to bring the distant white blur into focus, a wall of white coming toward him, swallowing tree-tops as it came. *Holy shit!*

He spun and raced back through the grove of trees, trying to stay ahead of the blizzard chasing him, but the wind was faster and he was soon enveloped in a perfect whiteout. Blinded, he stopped moving. There was no telling where he was now to the trees. He hadn't turned while running, so the slope had to lie behind him and the cliff face ahead, but one misstep too near a tree could be deadly. Unfortunately, just standing still wasn't an option either. In a blizzard this fierce, he would soon find himself buried, and unable to move at all. He carefully poked the snow ahead with his stick and slid one foot forward at a time, trying to feel his way forward. *I know I was nearly out of the trees and they were only 50 feet from the cliff. It's not far*, he told himself. *Just go slow.*

Poke, slide one foot, poke, slide the next. Then the snow fell out from under him. Slipping and sliding straight down, he instantly realized he'd stepped into a tree well. He kept sliding down and down with nothing to stop his plunge. Instinctively, he covered his face and head with his arms trying to trap a pocket of air as he fell. Maybe twenty feet down, he stopped sliding but dislodged snow slid down on top and around him, packing him in tightly as if being covered in liquid concrete, pinning him in place. He couldn't move one inch now. The snow muffled all outside sound so all he could hear was the panicked rhythm of his own heart and his lungs taking in what little air he'd managed to trap with him. He tried not to panic and breathe slowly, evenly.

For all the good that's going to do me, he thought. *Won't be long before my air runs out.*

He berated himself for his over-confidence, coming out here alone despite Eli's warnings. He knew better. The first rule of winter is always to travel with a buddy. *Lone wolves die alone.*

But Ronnie was injured and Eli refused to follow him, so he'd had no choice but to go alone. And now he was going to die for it. He wondered how long it would be before they found his body. Not before the spring thaw. He'd look pretty gruesome by then. He pictured Ronnie's face twisted in horror, that same look he wore when Jim gutted those fish they'd caught. Ronnie was squeamish about things like that. *Those were some good fish. We were having such a great trip till the weather turned on us.* He felt dizzy, his thoughts growing more disconnected. *So this is what it's like to suffocate. Weird.* He didn't even feel cold anymore, packed in snow like this. It would be a comfortable death. Odd that he wasn't scared either, just deeply sad that he couldn't say goodbye to his family. As his consciousness gradually faded, he envisioned Karen floating before him, her hand reaching. He wanted so badly to reach back.

Sharp pain stabbed into one of the arms over his head. He felt himself being pulled upward and fresh air rushed over his face. He sucked it into his lungs. As his vision cleared, he looked up to see the muzzle of a huge bear clamped over his arm, dragging him to the surface.

It's Grizzy. Grizzy's got me.

The bear continued pulling until he was up and away from the tree well, then let go. As Jim lay there gasping for air, the bear stood over him, butting him with his nose, grunting impatiently.

"Okay, okay." Jim pushed the gigantic head of the bear aside and sat up. His left arm ached where Grizzy had sunk his teeth into it. "Let me catch my breath, dammit." Grizzy snorted in his face. "Ugh," Jim grimaced and turned aside to suck in another lungful of clean fresh air. Rather than get another whiff of Grizzy's bear breath, he tried to stand but found himself up to his waist in deep snow. His snowshoes had been lost either in the fall or the rescue, traversing even a short distance would be a huge physical challenge and there was more snow still falling.

He looked around trying to get his bearings. Fortunately, the whiteout that nearly claimed his life had cleared enough that he could see the soaring cliff face. Just as he'd thought, he'd nearly been free of the pines before sliding into that tree well, but the snowshoe tracks he'd counted on for leading him back to the hidden opening had been obliterated, covered by a deep layer of fresh snow. With no visual sign of where the opening was, he guessed it lay straight ahead. He tried to move in that direction, feet sinking in so deeply that he had to do a half-crawl swim to make any headway. The bear watched him struggle. After advancing merely a few feet, he had to stop to catch his breath again and wipe the sweat from his forehead before it froze on his skin. Grizzy moved up alongside him and growled, looking over his shoulder at him. Remembering Eli's story of riding the bear to safety, he asked, "Is that an invitation?" he asked.

The bear grunted and blew air without moving. Taking that as a 'yes', Jim cautiously lay one hand on the bear's side. No reaction. Then both hands. Still nothing. "Okay. I'm climbing aboard. Please don't kill me." He slid his arms up over Grizzy's back and pulled himself up until he could throw a leg over to the other side and sit up. Once settled, the bear ambled forward without complaint. Jim shook his head in disbelief. "No one's ever going to believe this."

To his surprise, the bear turned sharply to the left as they approached the cliff, then quickly found the entrance. When he climbed onto the rocky ledge, the bear stopped and looked back at him. Jim got the message and slid off. Grizzy grunted again then squeezed ahead through the passage.

As Jim followed the bear, he recognized that this was the same as what Eli had experienced. Without this bear's intervention, they both would have died. Eli from exposure and his returning illness, and Jim from suffocation in a snow-packed tree well. Even if he hadn't fallen into it, without his tracks left to follow, there was a good chance he would never have found his way back to the hidden entrance. Even from only feet away, the opening had been virtually invisible. If not for this strange bear, he'd be dead. It was a sobering realization.

When he and the bear exited the rocky maze into the warm green valley, Eli was there waiting for them. He watched Jim knock snow off his pants and boots, then peel off the heavy winter jacket, gloves, and hat, all of which were thickly covered in white. Jim looked down at his shirt sleeve covering the forearm Grizzy had clamped onto to pull him from certain death, expecting to see it blood-soaked, but the fabric revealed no evidence of injury. Probably just bruised then.

"So how was it out there?" Eli asked.

"Bit raw," Jim replied not willing to admit how right Eli's warnings had been.

"Raw, huh? Sort of like your face, then," Eli said.

Jim brought a hand to his cheek and winced. He saw blood on his fingertips. The ice-filled wind must have scraped the exposed skin off his face like a sandblaster.

"Best treat that with my healing balm. Once you get your breath back, that is," he added with a knowing smirk as he glanced at the bear. Jim narrowed his eyes. How could Eli know he'd nearly suffocated in a tree well?

"Did you follow me?" Jim asked.

Eli shook his head. "Nope. Been waitin right here the whole time. I'm not dressed for the cold like Grizzy here."

Grizzy grunted in response to his name, then shook himself like a wet dog, sending melting snow and ice flying in all directions.

As Eli and the bear ambled off together, Jim wondered not for the first time, just how much the two could communicate with each other.

Chapter 19
Old Red's Heart Attack

November 12, 1973

They flew every day that weather permitted—searching from dawn to dusk—some days barely making it back to Anchorage before the weather shut them out or they ran low on fuel. Several times a sudden change forced them to land in Talkeetna or Matanuska Valley to spend the night.

The daily search affected them all in different ways. Karen and Pattie both lost weight and Old Red looked even more haggard than usual. Jamie however thrived on the adventure, eagerly sitting up front with binoculars, and peppering Red with questions. He just knew he would be the one to find his dad.

Jamie had been learning to fly from his dad in the Cessna, it had dual controls and his dad let him fly for a while each time they had gone up over the last few years. Jim had even talked him through a few landings with Jamie handling the controls without help. Although the minimum age for a private pilot license is 17, Jim knew Jamie would be qualified long before that.

Jamie paid close attention to the way Old Red flew the big Norseman. This airplane had only one control wheel on the left side so Jamie couldn't help Old Red fly—He wished he could, as it was obvious Old Red was really tired and didn't look well.

Search and rescue, Civil Air Patrol, and several of Jim's pilot friends had been searching for weeks, as the weather permitted, to no avail. There was just no sign of them or their aircraft.

They were returning to Anchorage after a long day fighting turbulence over the mountainous terrain. The wind tossed them about as if on a boat in a stormy sea. Despite the constraint of their seat belts and shoulder harnesses, it slammed them against the overhead and threw them against the side doors.

The girls gripped each other's hands and shared wide-eyed looks. Pattie got sick and tossed up her lunch in the barf bag she found in the seat back. Karen tried to put on a brave face for Pattie, but even she had never experienced this frightening a flight.

Old Red continued fighting the controls to keep the airplane level. Karen was alarmed to see that he was sweating profusely and turning pale. "We have to get out of here, it's just too rough today. I'm afraid we might damage the airplane in this stuff. I'm turning around."

Karen was the first to notice how Old Red looked. From her seat behind Jamie, she could clearly see his face

"Red," she asked, "are you okay?"

"I don't know. Not feelin so good. Can't focus and I'm getting this pain in my chest. Don't know if…if I can—" He clutched his chest, a grimace on his face. Then his head fell forward, his body held upright only by his shoulder harness.

"Red!" Jamie exclaimed. The plane tilted, and he reached over to grab the wheel. "Mom, I think he's having a heart attack or something."

"Red! Red!" Karen shouted, but there was no response.

Jamie couldn't reach the controls to stabilize the plane from the passenger seat, and the strong winds and turbulence tossed them around.

"Oh my god!" Pattie cried out, "We're going to die." There was a look of sheer terror on her face.

"Jamie, can you fly this thing?" Karen asked.

"I think so. But I have to get into his seat."

Karen put a hand on Pattie's arm and took a breath. "Okay, we'll have to pull him out of the way. Jamie, try to hold this thing level. Pattie, you need to help me get Red unbuckled. We'll pull him into the back with us, so Jamie can take over."

Karen unbuckled herself and reached forward, but Pattie just sat there, eyes wide, frozen with fear.

"Pattie, move!" Karen yelled, startling her into action. Pattie grabbed Red's arm.

Jamie unbuckled his harness and was immediately thrown on top of Red. He pushed off to let his mom unbuckle the unconscious Red.

Karen was out of her seat trying to reach Red's harness. The plane bounced, and she was thrown sideways, banging her head on the bulkhead, cutting her scalp. She felt something wet trickling down the side of her face.

Pattie shrieked. "Oh my God, Karen, you're bleeding!"

"Never mind that, help me with Red."

Jamie gripped the wheel hard to level out. A short lull in the turbulence gave the women the chance they needed. Using almost superhuman strength, they dragged Red out of Jamie's way and pulled him between the two front seats back with them.

Jamie climbed into the empty pilot seat, strapped himself in, and slid the seat adjustment full forward.

"You got this?" Karen asked her son.

"Yeah, Mom, I got it. You okay?"

"I'm okay."

"How is he?"

"Still breathing," She buckled him in and checked his pulse, steady and slow. "Do you know how to get us back to Anchorage?"

"Yeah, I've flown this way a bunch of times with Dad. I'll call the tower and let them know we're coming."

"Okay. Good. Tell them to have an ambulance waiting. You think you can land this thing?"

"I think so. I watched Old Red real close and it doesn't feel much different from the Cessna. Dad had me landing that pretty well. I should be fine."

"Okay. We're counting on you."

"Yeah, no kidding." He rolled his eyes at the obvious.

When they flew out of the mountainous terrain, the turbulence finally died down. Jamie got on the radio and let the tower know their situation. Pattie still looked glazed with fright and Karen patted her arm in reassurance.

Coming in for the landing on Lake Hood, Jamie talked back and forth with the tower. He copied the same airspeed and power settings that he'd seen Red use. Gliding over the trees of the Lake Hood shoreline, he slowed the airplane and lifted the nose into a gentle flare above the frozen lake. The skis touched down smoothly, and he pulled the power back to idle, letting the airplane coast to a stop. The ambulance and paramedics were already racing towards them across the frozen lake, red flashing lights reflecting off the ice. Jamie shut down the engine and let out a long-held breath. He twisted in his seat to look back at his mom and Pattie and grinned.

Karen shook her head in amazement. "You did it."

Pattie sat staring straight ahead, frozen in her seat. "I thought we were all going to die."

"Sorry to disappoint you," Jaimie said, wearing that shit-eating grin.

Pattie focused on him, then grabbed hold of his face, kissing his cheek repeatedly. "Oh my god, Jaimie. Thank you, thank you so much. You saved us. You're my hero!"

He stiffened in embarrassment, a hot color rising in his face, and squirmed to get free, but she had him in her grip.

Seeing the ambulance pulling up, Karen released her harness, opened the side door, and jumped out to meet the paramedics. "He's there in the back. I think it's a heart attack."

When the paramedics rushed inside to attend to Red, Pattie finally released Jamie and climbed out of the plane to follow Karen.

Chapter 20
Karen with Old Red

November 14, 1973

Red didn't die, much to Karen's relief, but he needed to stay in the hospital for a few days. The doctors told her they wanted to run some tests before he could leave. It might be a week or more before he would be released. That meant they couldn't use Red's plane to keep searching for Jim and Ronnie on their own. They would have to rely on the official search and rescue efforts which so far had come up empty.

"He's fortunate to have family nearby. So many of our elderly patients don't," the young lady in admissions said.

"Oh, we're not related," Karen replied.

"Mr. Wilson is your husband's grandfather"

"Pardon me?"

"I understand Mr. Wilson has been staying with you recently. Is that right?"

Karen covered her surprise. "Yes, he has." Her brain whirled at the revelation of Red's legal name. Red was James Wilson, Sr.—Jim's ostracized grandfather? Jim had mentioned him only once, back when they were still dating, to tell her they had cut ties long ago—some unforgivable family issue.

Filled with questions, Karen went to Red's room. He wasn't awake and looked deathly pale, and weak. No longer the obnoxious, smelly, belligerent drunk who'd made a pass at her only a few weeks ago. A monitor on the wall made a quiet beeping sound as his heartbeat drew a spikey line scrolling across the screen. Seeing him lying there with an oxygen mask and hooked up to tubes running to an IV, catheter, and BP machine, she knew he was in no condition to undergo an interrogation. Karen stared at his face looking for any resemblance to her husband. Maybe the nose. Hard to tell under these conditions.

She remembered her first impression of Old Red, a drunk old pervert, who tried hitting on her and Patty. What kind of man was she dealing with?

When she went to the hospital the next day to talk to Red, she found him sitting up in bed. His color looked good and when he told her they were getting ready to discharge him, she made up her mind to start asking hard questions. She sat in the visitor seat, crossed her arms, and frowned at him.

"Looking forward to getting back to that nice quiet little room of yours," he said, oblivious to her pose and hardened expression. "Just need to keep these little white pills with me, in case it happens again," Old Red held up a small green bottle. "Nitroglycerin—what they use to blow up mines. Hard to believe they could turn the stuff into a pill to make a heart work proper."

"I'm starting to think it'll take more than pills to fix yours."

Red looked at her then and scowled. "Somethin' botherin' you, girl?"

"I don't appreciate being lied to, Mr. James Wilson. Sr!"

Red shifted uncomfortably and dropped his gaze. "So, Jimmy's told you about me?"

"No. Not a word. I figure you must have done something pretty despicable to be cut out of the lives of the men who carry your name. Are you a murderer, a pedophile, or what?"

Old Red gaped at her, speechless for a moment. "What? No. I never… what the hell has Jimmie been telling you?"

"Nothing. That's the point. He won't talk about it. What exactly did you do?"

Red shook his head and sighed. "It's more about what I didn't do than what I did. Can't change the past."

"I don't like keeping a man under my roof that my husband despises. So either you explain yourself, or we're done here."

"Okay. I want to help. I do. I owe Jimmy that." Red frowned and ran a hand over the top of his gray head, then clasped both hands together in his lap. He couldn't seem to meet her eyes. "Haven't talked to anyone about this in a long time. Don't even like thinking about it, to be honest." He took another long breath. "The bad feelings between me and my son started when Junior was just seventeen. I taught him how to fly and figured he might take over the business one day, but I wanted him to graduate high school and go to college first, something I never got to do. He was all for it, till he met that Inuit girl and got her pregnant. He wanted to marry her and live with her in that village of hers, but seeing as he wasn't much more than a kid himself, I said no and threatened to ship him off to military school. That's when he ran off to be with her. When I went after him to bring him home, everyone in that village said he wasn't there even though I knew he was. Went back more than a few times, and even took the trooper with me, but Junior wouldn't show his face, and the people there just kept lying, saying he wasn't there. Those people stole my son and turned him against me, so I stopped taking their trades and bringing them supplies. Told them they could all starve or freeze to death for all I cared. A year went by. No word from my son. Then the attack on Pearl Harbor happened. Junior came to me not long after and said he was being drafted. The government had him down as over 18, unmarried, zero dependents, and out of school – prime army material."

"So they never married?" she asked.

"Not in the eyes of the law. Just some native ceremony. Before he left, he asked me to keep an eye on her and the kid and make sure they got what they needed. Said I would, of course, make him feel better, but…" Red fell silent again.

"But you didn't."

"No, I didn't. I never looked in on them. I didn't want anything to do with her or her people. I felt betrayed. I'd befriended them, traded with them for years, and then they took my son from me. Apparently, at some point, she contracted tuberculosis. She should have gone to a hospital, but instead, she relied on their *witch doctor*. And she died" He said the last with a twisted mouth.

"You mean their shaman," Karen corrected, mildly offended.

He blew air and shrugged. "Yeah. Right. Their shaman. Anyway, Junior never came back from the war.

"If I'd gotten her the help she needed when she needed it, she'd probably still be alive. I made him a promise and I broke it. The result is, that she died and Jimmy lost his mom and dad. That's a hard one to get around."

Karen nodded in agreement. Jim seldom mentioned the Inuit mother he'd lost at the age of eight, but whenever he did, she could see the pain in his eyes. With his father away, flying bombers somewhere over Europe, Jim and his mother had only each other. Many of the survival skills he'd learned from her, as well as countless stories. As an adult, Jim attended church with Karen and their son, but underneath Jim's Christian faith lay a bedrock of native legends and a deep connection to the people with whom he had lived during those early years. The only grandfather Jim acknowledged was the Inuit one who had fathered his mother. Old Red wasn't him.

Chapter 21
Christmas

December 24, 1973

With Old Red grounded, Pattie and Karen had to rely on Search and Rescue to find their lost husbands. The weeks went by turning into months with no sightings of the missing men or wreckage, and the search missions had dwindled to only a few flights weekly. Karen and Pattie had to keep bugging everyone they knew who owned a plane to keep searching. They could cling to hope as long as whatever had happened to their husbands remained a question mark. During Karen's last call to the Search and Rescue office, the expert there told her by now any wreckage would be long buried under the snow and there was little chance of finding any evidence of Jim's plane before spring thaw. They were officially calling off the search.

When Christmas rolled around, Karen invited Pattie to go with her to church to pray. "Maybe I'm crazy, but I feel in my heart they're still alive."

"Me too. I keep imagining them holed up somewhere, waiting out the winter until they can come back to us. I'll go to the service with you and afterward, let's come back to my place. We'll have a drink and toast to our husbands, wherever they are, wish them luck, and send them our love. I don't care what anybody says. Until someone proves otherwise, I say Ronnie and Jim are alive and well. I have to believe they're out there somewhere, just biding their time, and planning on how to get back to us." Karen and Pattie went to Christmas service to mourn their lost loved ones.

Afterward, "Let's go to my place and have that Christmas drink to our husbands, wherever they are. Wish them luck and love, and pray they come home safe and soon." Said Pattie.

***

"Cooked up somethin' special seein' as what day it is," Eli announced as he walked into their cave home carrying a gigantic wooden tray of sizzling food.

Jim shared a puzzled look with Ronnie. "What day would that be?"

Eli set the food down in the middle of the table and shook his head. "Guess you boys ain't been payin attention. Got my calendar right over there, plain as day."

Jim walked over to take a look at Eli's complicated calendar system etched into the cave wall. He pointed to one block of numbers, "Must be November something by now. Is it Thanksgiving?"

"Ha. You have lost track. No, we're over here, in December, late December. It's Christmas Eve." Eli thumped the date on the wall with his finger. "Come eat. This fish is gonna cool off fast."

"We missed Thanksgiving?" Ronnie asked as he pulled wooden plates from a shelf. "That sucks."

"It was a month ago and you were delirious with a fever. Be grateful you're alive to celebrate Christmas." Eli scolded him.

"I am, sure, but... I just happen to like Thanksgiving. Turkey, stuffing, sweet potatoes, pumpkin pie." He sighed and licked his lips.

"Well, you ain't getting none of that. You're gettin' fresh caught fish with plenty of taters and greens from the garden. I don't want to hear no complaints."

"No, this is great, Eli," Jim interrupted the exchange. "Thank you." He carried a plate over to the table to serve himself, then stared in amazement at the giant slab of fish that lay there, surrounded by roasted potatoes, green beans, onions, and carrots. Even with its head and tail missing, the char-broiled filet measured over four feet in length. "Is that a king salmon? Must have been huge."

"Oh, that's less than half of it. They grow really big in that lake below us here. Grizzy ate the rest of it but left us this part. Seein' as he's the one who caught it, seems only fair."

Jim had seen king salmon weighing well over 100 pounds and nearly as long as he was tall, but if this was less than half, Eli was talking about a monster fish eight or more feet in length. "So Grizzy hunts down in that underground lake?"

"No, he don't like it much down there. Stays away mostly, but he'll catch 'em when they come up to the surface, trying to swim up our stream here to escape whatever's after 'em."

That gave Jim pause, trying to picture what might panic an eight-foot fish.

"Come on now. Eat up!" Eli ordered. "There's plenty more where that came from."

The men filled their plates and sat down to eat. The fish tasted even better than it smelled. Each man ate everything on his plate and went back for seconds and even thirds.

Ronnie finally leaned back with a satisfied groan. "I can't eat another bite. Never thought I'd spend a Christmas Eve like this." He hesitated, scowling. "Funny. I just had the strangest feeling, like the girls were thinking about us. Having a drink to wish us a safe return. Weird, but it makes me feel good to think of them like that. I hope they're doing all right."

"I'm sure they're fine, "Jim said. "Worried about us, maybe, but fine."

The men shared worried looks followed by a long period of silence.

Jim lifted his mug in the air. "If you're right about them drinking to us, we should do the same. To our wives, and my son. May they stay safe."

"To Karen. To Pattie. To Jamie," the two said in overlapping toasts as they each raised a mug and clinked them together.

Eli watched them. "Sorry you boys are worried about your women seeing as you're stuck here with me, but I have to admit that I don't mind it so much. Been a long time since I could celebrate Christmas with another human being. Hope you boys won't mind that I made you each a little something to mark the occasion."

Jim scowled, uncomfortable to be on the receiving end. "I hope you didn't go to any trouble. You've already done more for us than we can ever repay."

"Now don't make a fuss. Did it more for my satisfaction than yours. Just something I felt like doin." Eli handed Ronnie and Jim each a little rawhide pouch, tied at the top. "Go on now, take a look."

Jim opened his pouch and pulled out a beautifully detailed gold bear hanging from a rawhide lanyard. "Eli, this is amazing." He turned the small golden bear over to look at it from all sides admiring the realistic fur and life-like pose. "

"Holy crap!" exclaimed Ronnie as he pulled out a matching bear. "You made these? Wow, Dude, this is primo."

"I can't believe the detail," Jim rubbed his thumb over the polished metal surface, taking in its bright yellow color. "Ely, is this gold?"

"Yep, pure gold."

"No. I can't accept this. You shouldn't be giving us this. It's got to be worth a lot."

"Oh, ain't nothin' much to me. I pull plenty of nuggets out of the stream. I use em for makin bullets seein as I ain't got no lead."

"You're kidding."

"Nope." Eli stepped over to the mantle next to where his rifle sat propped grabbed another pouch and dumped out a dozen round balls, all in gleaming gold. "Turns out gold works real well, and since it's harder than lead, they don't smash flat so I can reuse 'em over and over after I dig 'em out of whatever I shoot."

Jim wasn't sure whether to believe him. "Takes a lot of heat to melt gold. Heck of a lot more than lead."

"Yeah, don't I know it. In my younger days, I cooked up lead bullets over an open fire. To use the gold I had to build a kiln. Took a lot of figurin' out how to make it and create molds, but now I got it all down to a science. Be glad to show you how it's done, if you like. Anyway, I thought the bears were fittin' for you to have as a keepsake, seein as it was Grizzy who led me to you boys out there."

Jim and Ronnie followed Elis' gaze over to Grizzy who lifted his massive head from the floor to stare back at them. Jim remembered how the bear had also pulled him out of that suffocating tree well. He wondered again if Eli knew about that.

"Real gold," Ronnie said reverently as he stared at the small bear in his palm. "And you say there's lots of it? You never mentioned finding gold here before."

"Didn't trust you to know about it before. I've seen how that damned yellow metal can twist men's minds. Stuff's no big deal to me, seein' as I can't spend it out here and I ain't never gonna live nowhere else's. But you boys are planning on goin back home to your wives. Back to civilization where gold can change a man's life. So I'm leavin' it up to you. Take as much as you like. Much as you can carry. Just remember, no matter how much you have, it'll never be worth more than your lives, so keep that in mind."

***

Karen felt a shiver run down her spine and jumped up. "Pattie, I just had the strangest feeling, like the guys were acknowledging our Christmas toast and telling me they were alright. That was weird, but somehow I know it was a message from them."

Chapters 22
Waiting for breakup

March 1, 1974

Jim's short but nearly fatal excursion outside the sheltered valley convinced him they would need to wait for spring thaw before trying to return home.

With no place to go, Jim and Ronnie tried to find positive ways to pass the time. Something they both found of interest was Eli who was bound and determined to teach them skills forgotten to most folks of their own time. He showed them how to make gunpowder and how to load, prime, and fire the big flintlock rifle. He showed them how he made the golden bullets, really Minnie balls, using his hand-made forge.

They learned candle making using bear fat, how to make moose jerky, and even how to make paint from roots, berries, and even blood.

Eli had shown them his way to dress a kill, treat the hide, and make buckskin for shirts and pants. He even showed them how to make pemmican rations for travel, just like they used in the Civil War. They learned how to make a bow and arrows, as well as which plants and herbs were edible. These things had been common knowledge years ago but were all new to Jim and Ronnie. They stayed busy every day, learning skills, working the garden, or going with Eli to check his trap lines. They constructed pack frames from wood and bone and the packs from buckskin.

They even made buckskin shirts and pants to replace their torn and ragged clothes from the crash and trek, and fur hats.

Dressing in their new buckskin outfits they paraded for Eli's approval. "How do we look Eli?" asked Ronnie.

"You two are starting to look almost normal. Looks like a good fit, and will last a lot longer than those store-bought duds you were wearing."

All to get ready for the day they would venture out to make it home again!

When it wasn't a blizzard outside, they hunted with Eli, looking for moose or caribou for their meat and hides.

One day Eli took Jim and Ronnie down to the warm stream that ran through the hidden valley, showing them the rocky pools that contained the larger gold nuggets. They took off their boots, rolled up their pants legs, and wadded into the warm water gathering up nuggets.

Eli had made them each a rawhide pouch with a drawstring top that they filled with nuggets. Some of the larger ones were the size of their thumb.

"Wow dude," Exclaimed Ronnie, "This must be what it felt like when Sutter found all that gold that started the California gold rush. I can't wait to take some home to Pattie."

Evenings were usually spent soaking their tired bodies in the crystal-hot pools, where they relaxed and shared stories of their lives. The guys were fascinated by Eli's stories of living in the 1800s and fighting in the civil war. Stories of overwhelming hardships he'd endured in his long and colorful life kept them spellbound and asking for more. The grief of losing his family and the loneliness he must have felt all these years tore at their hearts.

On the other hand, Ely had a hard time believing their stories of modern life with computers, TV, microwave ovens, and modern jet airplanes. Modern medicine, heart transplants, and artificial limbs were especially hard for him to comprehend. "I ain't so sure you fellas are not just kiddin' with me. I never heard of stuff like that, ever. Not so sure I believe ya, but they're good stories anyway." Eli said, grinning and shaking his head with a twinkle in his eye.

Well healed from their injuries, Jim and Ronnie grew stronger each day. Jim credited their new-found endurance to all the manual labor and fresh food. Ronnie thought it had something more to do with Eli's blue tea. Whatever the explanation, they were confident they would be in great shape to tackle the return trip home when the time came.

One evening as they were cleaning up after dinner, a rumbling sounded in the distance, growing louder until the ground under their feet swayed, and their plates slid across the table. Jim grabbed one before it fell off the edge.

"Earthquake!" Ronnie yelled as he dropped to the floor and rolled underneath the table to grip its legs. "Get under here, Dude!"

Jim stayed put, keeping Eli's mugs and plates from falling. The swaying ceased and the rumbling slowly faded away. He leaned down to look at Ronnie. "It's over. You can come out now."

Ronnie gave him a dirty look and got out from under the table. "You should listen to me, man. You never know how bad they'll get. I'm from California and we train for these things in school. Duck and cover, okay?"

"Uh-huh. We get plenty of them here in Alaska, too. We're all on that same ring of fire."

Grizzy, who'd been lying on the floor snoring just before the earthquake hit, sniffed the air then suddenly stood on his back legs and roared.

"Go! Go!" Eli ran at them with Grizzy in hot pursuit.

That startled Jim into action. The three men and bear galloped out the cave entrance. He went to close the wooden door, but Eli stopped him.

"No, stay clear." He waved them back just as dust billowed out the open doorway mixed with clouds of steam.

Jim felt the superheated air radiating toward him and backed away It smelled strongly of sulfur.

"What the hell's going on?" Ronnie danced backward.

"It's the hot springs actin' up. Don't happen often, but when it does you gotta move fast." The heat dissipated as Eli spoke and a cool breeze followed. "It's over. Should be safe now."

Jim looked at Ronnie in horror, realizing they could have been boiled alive if an eruption like this had occurred while they'd been soaking in those hot pools below. He took a breath and controlled his emotions before saying the obvious. "Eli! You should have warned us."

"Ain't no big deal. The mountain rumbles and shakes a bit now and again, but then things quiet back down. And Grizzy here always lets me know if there's a problem."

Jim regarded the bear again. Just how many times was this bear going to save his life?

Grizzy met Jim's stare with an expression that almost seemed to imply "As many times as it takes."

Chapter 23
The map

March 15, 1974

Near the middle of March, outside Eli's protected valley, the snow still lay deep and the streams remained stubbornly frozen. Even with perfect conditions, the journey home on foot would be a huge undertaking, but Jim wondered if waiting for better weather was wise. The ground tremors were growing more frequent and he'd noted animals in the valley displaying restlessness, many even leaving the enchanted valley, despite the icy winds and lack of food waiting for them outside. He suspected some instinct deep inside them sensed danger. Maybe they smelled the thermal pools growing hotter. Or spied tiny cracks and fissures in the cliffs from magma climbing up long-vacant tubes inside the mountain's core. Standing outside the door to Eli's cave home in the early morning, he stared up at the tallest peak where not a goat was to be seen and a thin ominous trail of dark smoke rose into the sky.

Fearing the worst, he went back inside the cave and made sure his and Ronnie's survival gear was packed and ready to grab at a moment's notice. His preparations did not go unobserved.

"I hope you're not plannin' on leavin' here before the river breaks up," Eli commented from the table where he sat crunching on some dried-up concoction he called cereal, something Jim hadn't been able to acquire a taste for.

"Not planning on it, but if that mountain of yours decides to blow, I want to be ready."

"She's just lettin' off a little steam is all."

"I hope you're right, but with all the trembling lately and animals leaving, I'm not so sure."

Eli gestured toward Grizzy, who lay splayed out on the floor, eyes closed and snoring. "I won't worry till he does."

Eli had spoken confidently, but that night he pulled out a small wooden brush of mink fur and some homemade paint, then spread out a thin supple sheet of buckskin and started drawing a map. "Seein' as you boys are fixin to leave here soon, I thought I should show you best as I can recollect of how I got here from Talkeetna."

"I was hoping you would show us the way out of here yourself," Ronnie said.

"Suppose I could for a little way, but you know I can't venture out too far for too long before my old sickness starts comin back on me. And just in case anythin should happen to me you should have a map to follow."

"Nothing's going to happen to you, Eli," Ronnie said. "You're strong as a horse and almost as big."

"Don't think I like the comparison much, not after seein' all those dead ones piled up along the gold trails. A terrible sight." Eli shook his head, chasing away the gruesome memory. "Nope, horses ain't much good out here. Not enough for them to eat, and the terrains too rough. They end up either starvin or breakin a leg. Come on over here so I can explain what you're lookin at."

Jim and Ronnie joined him at the table to look at the map he'd drawn.

"You'll need to follow these small streams down the mountainsides to the big river south of us here. Won't be easy goin'. Be sure to pack plenty of dried food and you'll need to supplement with game along the way. The streams will lead you." He pointed to his drawing showing where the threads of tributaries combined into a thick snaking line. "The big river runs west then curves south down to Talkeetna, the same way you need to go. If it's still frozen solid, you'll have to walk it, which means dealing with heaps of slabs and hillocks."

"Slabs and what?" Ronnie asked.

"Upheavals of river ice. If it's just startin' to break up, that's when it's most dangerous… expect thin spots and chunks of floating ice. If you're lucky, it'll be flowin' free by the time you reach it. In that case, you'll have to stop and build yourselves a raft like I showed ya. It means losin' some time, but you'll make it up easy by travelin' a whole lot faster. It goes wide as a lake in parts then narrows through canyons in others. There'll be rapids along the way, of course, especially in the drops and narrow canyons, but if the gods be willin' you'll make it."

"And which gods would those be?" Jim asked, genuinely curious.

Eli chuckled. "S'pose that's up for debate. I'm a half-Indian baptized Christian with a Swedish father who was a big fan of Odin."

"That's so cool," Ronnie said. "The son of a Viking."

Jim said. "My mother was Inuit. I lived with her in her village when I was a child and she taught me a lot."

"You're lucky then. I never knew my mother or her people," Eli said.

Jim and Eli nodded at each other, sharing the knowing looks of men who belonged to the same club.

Chapter 24
The big shake starts

March 28, 1974

On the morning of March 28, while Eli was tending his gardens and Jim and Ronnie were doing their daily work, the ground started to shake and undulate so violently it threw the men off their feet. Rocks skittered down the cliff sides surrounding them.

"Best get inside," Eli yelled, and they ran into the cave to wait it out. When the ground stopped shaking and the rumbling faded, they went back out to assess the damage. A boulder as big as a Jeep had rolled down through Eli's garden and uprooted a tree. Its roots stuck up into the air.

"I'm starting to feel like we've overstayed our welcome," Jim said.

Eli stared up at dark smoke curling up into the sky from the mountain's peak and nodded, "I'm starting to think you're right. Could be she wants you gone."

"She?" Ronnie asked.

"The mountain there. I think of her as a volcanic goddess, the daughter of Denali, the sacred one to local natives. Been takin care of me all these years while she's been peacefully sleeping. Shakin a little now and then but nothing serious. She seems a might upset now though. Shakin more than I can ever remember. She watches over this valley and guards it. Over the years, she's crushed a few unwanted intruders. You're the first she's let in since I came here."

Jim scowled at that. "You mean there were others who've tried?"

"Yup. I've found bodies. That's why I was worried about bringing you two in here, but it turned out all right. Either she couldn't smash you without getting me too or it had something to do with you being half-native like me. Whatever she was thinkin', I'm glad she let you boys stay here for a while, but I think she's had enough of you. It's time you went. I been noticin' some of the animals been leavin', reckon they can sense danger comin'. Those thermal pools seem to be getting hotter and I've spotted new cracks along the cliffside. Things just don't seem right"

Jim and Ronnie exchanged glances, both of them thinking the same thing… that the old man was a little looney!

"You should come with us," Ronnie said.

"No, this is my home. I can't live nowhere else no more. I'd just get sick on you so you're better off on your own."

"Eli, it's too dangerous to stay here. These tremors are building up to something big." Jim said.

"Don't worry. I'm pretty sure she'll calm down once you're gone." Eli pointed to their backpacks sitting next to the door. "You got everything you need there, including the map I drew ya?"

"We do," Jim replied, keeping himself from commenting on Ely's bizarre theories about the motives of a mountain.

As Jim and Ronnie hefted their backpacks onto their shoulders, Eli walked over to the back wall and lifted his flintlock down from above the mantle. "You best take this with you, too."

Jim lifted his palms and shook his head. "No, that's not necessary. I still have my handgun."

"Alright, I'll say my goodbyes then. Hope you boys make it out alive."

"We'll do our best." Jim looked out the open door, and took a long breath, preparing himself to cross the sanctuary of this protected valley and leave it all behind. "And I will try to come back someday."

"Me too," Ronnie said.

"Well, if'n you do, you'd be welcome."

"Oh hell," Ronnie said and threw his arms around Eli. "I'm going to miss you."

Eli allowed the hug for a long moment before shoving Ronnie away. "Go on now. Get out of here while you still can." When the pair still hesitated, Eli raised his voice. "I said get!" Eyes red and rubbing his nose, Eli turned away and walked back into his cave.

"Time to go," Jim said.

"I feel like shit leaving him here."

"I know. But we can't stay and he can't leave."

"Think it's true? That he can't leave?"

Jim shrugged. "He believes it's true, which is pretty much the same thing."

"Yeah. I guess." Ronnie sighed heavily.

Side by side, the pair headed for the maze that would lead them out of the valley but didn't get more than twenty feet before another low rumbling began again. The ground heaved under their feet, and they struggled to maintain their balance. The rumbling grew to the intensity of an oncoming freight train, the sound echoing off the surrounding cliffs. They looked up to see the cliff walls calving, sending huge slabs of dirt, rocks, and trees, all sliding downward, turning the green valley into a brown sea of rolling debris with a huge cloud of billowing dust rushing straight for them.

"Run!"

Jim and Ronnie spun around and sprinted hard back to the cave.

"Hurry!" Eli screamed holding the door open for them. The cloud of dust was at their heels.

When the two shot through, Eli slammed the door shut against the onrushing tide and threw the latch. The men and the bear backed away watching dust seep through the door's seams and under the sill. A second later, boulders crashed against it, splintering the wood. Clouds of dirt flew in through newly opened cracks and the latch and hinges started to splinter under the pressure threatening to give way any second.

"It's not going to hold." Jim coughed under his arm, trying to block the dust.

The bear roared and then galloped toward the tunnels leading below.

"Come on!" Eli yelled.

"But what about the hot pools? We could boil," Ronnie said.

"It's either that or get buried alive. Choose your poison, boys." Not waiting for an answer, Eli ran down into the tunnels after Grizzy.

"Go!" Jim pushed Ronnie ahead of him. "We need to get past the pools before they gas up." Though burdened with the weight of their backpacks filled with essential survival gear, the pair dashed after Eli and ran hard.

The ground trembled beneath their pounding feet throwing them against the walls. The strong smell of sulfur in the warming air alerted Jim to impending disaster. "Get down!" he yelled and shoved Ronnie flat. "Take cover!" Face down they buried their heads inside their arms and the furred hoods of their parkas, screaming as superheated sulfuric steam rushed over them. The blast lasted only seconds, but it felt like forever before enough cool clean air followed that they could lift their sweat-beaded faces.

"You okay?" Jim asked.

"I think so. Slightly parboiled maybe." Ronnie got to his feet and then pointed at the steam rising from Jim's back. "Your pack looks fried."

"Yeah, yours, too. Better the packs than us. Come on," Jim said. Though worried their gear might be damaged, this was no time to check on it.

Red-faced and coughing from inhaled sulfur, the two men started running again, down and down through the rocky tunnels, past the glowworm-lit caverns, and on into the cave with the hot pools that had just nearly steamed them alive. The pools' bubbling waters had taken on an ominous red hue, looking like springs from hell now rather than soothing blue-green spas. In the rising steam, the painted figures on the cave walls seemed to wriggle, dance, and point to the hidden door to the carved staircase that would take them down to the great underground lake. When they reached the door, they found it standing open.

"Looks like Eli and Grizzy made it, too." Ronnie stood in the open doorway and sniffed gratefully at the cool air coming up from below but hesitated to go down.

"What's the hold-up?"

"Just feels like we're heading for a dead-end."

"Not like we've got a choice. The way back is blocked, and these pools will kill us if we don't get below them. Keep moving. We'll figure something out."

Ronnie nodded and started down the curving stairwell. "You're right, we'll figure it out. Maybe it's not a dead end. I mean, Eli admitted he doesn't know where the lake goes, right? Maybe we can finish building the raft and see what's across the lake?"

Standing with his arms crossed at the bottom, Eli watched them descend. "Took your sweet time. I thought I was gonna have to send Grizzy up to rescue you."

"No need." Jim offloaded his steamed backpack at the bottom of the stairs. The brisk air of the icy cave cooled his seared skin, but the glowing blue water of the lake looked like an even better tonic so he started toward it. Grizzy cut him off.

"Get out of the way, bear."

"He's just trying to protect you," Eli said. "If you need to wash off, come over here where it's shallow."

Jim shook his head in annoyance, but said, "Fine." He went over to where Eli pointed to a small inlet between some boulders where the water was only inches deep. There Jim splashed cold water on his face and hands, feeling instant relief.

Ronnie joined him and did the same. "Oh man, that feels so much better." The stinging was already gone. "What is it about this place, Eli? I mean how does it heal us like this?"

"Can't explain how it works. Just know it does." Eli sat down on one of the boulders nearby on the sand. "Well, boys, looks like we're stuck here for a while, but there's food and plenty of water, so things could be a whole lot worse."

"I thought your mountain wanted us gone," Jim said. "Guess she changed her mind again."

Eli chuckled. "I guess she did. Ain't that just like a woman?"

Ronnie looked up at the icy blue ceiling above them. "You think its safe staying in here? I remember them saying at the Mendenhall ice caves that these things can melt and collapse when it warms up."

"Maybe so, but this ain't no ordinary ice cave," Eli replied. "It's like the valley up there. It never changes."

"This isn't natural," Jim said, "Any more than those wall paintings, stone stairs, and that big door at the top of them. Someone did a lot of work in here over many years for some reason."

"Someone or something," Eli said in a low voice. "Maybe you should take a closer look at those paintings."

Jim wondered if this was more of Eli's delusions, like the personification of the mountain, but kept that thought to himself.

Chapter 25
Trapped at the lake

April 1, 1974

Trapped deep below the surface, Jim and Ronnie had explored every inch of the cavern they could reach looking for a possible way out. Jim paced the length of the waterfront, dragging his feet to make patterns in the glittering sand. As he looked at the gold flecks, he fingered the little bear hanging from the cord around his neck He glanced over at Eli sitting atop a boulder with his legs crossed like a yogi staring out across the water.

"Have you taken a good look at those paintings yet?" Eli waved back at the 100-foot-tall rock wall supporting the stone staircase that curved down from the cavern's entrance onto the sand-covered beach.

Jim frowned. "I've seen them."

"No, I mean a really good look. Go on, look closer."

"Fine." Jim sighed and wandered over to the paintings decorating the rocky wall. Among the hundreds of indecipherable white spirals, radiating circles, and hash marks were recognizable representations of animals. He could identify caribou, moose, and bear among the land animals, sharks, and killer whales among the ocean dwellers and what looked strangely enough like a dinosaur, or the lock Ness monster.

A whale figure with sharp teeth reminded him of a killer whale petroglyph he'd seen among the engraved stones of

Wrangell, Alaska. That small chunk of coastline had the highest concentration of petroglyphs in the world, thus justifying its name, Petroglyph Beach. Archaeologists dated those etchings close to 8,000 years old. The theory was that the petroglyphs were made by the Tlingit tribe native to the area, but none of their descendants living today knew what those images had intended to communicate.

To see the higher ones he backed up. What they meant was anyone's guess. *Could be anything from hunting site markers to religious symbols to… wait. What the hell is that?*

"Hey, Ronnie. Come over here and look at this."

Jim pointed a finger outlining a huge overall shape so large he hadn't recognized it as a single cohesive figure until now. "Does that look like what I think it does?"

Ronnie squinted at the individual symbols for a moment, then his eyes widened as he took in the entirety of all that he saw, and his mouth opened. "Whoa. No way, dude."

Both men instinctively took another step back.

The individual symbols and pictorial representations had been arranged to create one massive humanoid figure—a giant man wearing boots and what appeared to be a visor helmet like an astronaut or deep-sea diver.

"Took you, boys, long enough," Eli smirked wryly from his perch on the boulder.

"You knew this was here? Why didn't you tell us?" Jim asked.

He scoffed. "You already think I've got a screw loose. No, better you should see it for yourselves."

Ronnie leaned closer to Jim and lowered his voice to a whisper. "Did you ever see that movie about *ancient astronauts*?"

Jim nodded, knowing the film Ronnie meant— 'Chariots of the Gods', a cheesy documentary he'd found ridiculous and had said so when he'd watched it with his son.

"What do you think it means?"

"Probably just somebody's over-active imagination. Or a joke." Jim looked meaningfully at Eli and spoke louder. "This your doing, old man?"

Eli glared back. "Shoulda figured you'd see it that way. Don't know why I even bother." Scowling, Ely turned his back to them again and faced the water.

Ronnie tugged at Jim's sleeve and whispered again. "Come on. How could he have done all of this? Those steps are solid granite slabs and the way they're worn it looks like they've been here for hundreds of years with lots of foot traffic.

"Unless his whole story's just something he made up? You really believe he's 125 years old?" asked Jim.

"Yeah, Dude. That's exactly what I believe. Makes more sense than what you're saying."

Jim blew air from his lungs and shook his head. "It just doesn't make sense. None of this does!"

"Maybe you need to smoke some weed, man. Open your mind."

Jim snorted. "Maybe you smoked so much, your brain fell out."

Ronnie scowled at him. "I'm not stupid. You think I'm stupid?!"

"No, I... I didn't mean that. I just—" Jim paused.

"I'm the one who handles all the inventory. I do the math, remember? "Ronnie retorted.

"I know, I know. I don't want to fight with you. This is a crazy place and it's making me crazy trying to make sense of it" Jim went on.

Ronnie nodded and took a slow breath. "Yeah, I get that."

After listening to their conversation Eli said,

"First of all, no, I did not build those stairs or the door to them. They were here long before me. The same goes for these here painted pictures. Don't know who did it or why or what for. Your guess is as good as mine. As for the gold... take all you want, all you can carry, take it all for all I care. Don't do me a bit of good. Can't eat it, can't spend it. So what do I need it for? Not a goldarn thing, ceptin' the bullets I hunt with."

Jim was about to offer further argument when the ground trembled under their feet and a chunk of ice fell from the great height of the cavern ceiling and splashed into the water.

"We can't wait around like this. This whole place could come down on our heads. I say we finish that old raft of yours and see if there's a way out at the other end of this lake."

"That she-devil of a mountain's gonna calm down eventually. We got plenty enough food and water to last us. When she stops her fussin', we can dig our way out again. Could take a while, o'course, but—"

"Yeah, like days, weeks, months even," Jim said. "And that's assuming these earthquakes ever stop."

As if to punctuate Jim's worries, the ground trembled again. "I'm going to finish that raft."

Eli sighed. "Some folks just gotta keep learnin' things the hard way."

Jim ignored the jab – a reminder of his ill-fated solo beyond the valley which resulted in his needing to be rescued by Grizzy. *This time is different,* he told himself. *Me and Ronnie are both good swimmers and there's no risk of freezing, falling off a cliff, or running into a snowstorm.*

Eli agreed to help, even though he refused to go along with them, so they all set out to finish the long-neglected raft.

Working together, within a few days they had a proper raft strapped together with rawhide, two paddles, and a tiller. It felt good to be doing something constructive rather than just waiting around for whatever happened next. They didn't know how long it would take to reach the end of this lake. A day, two, more? Not that there was any way to tell time down here. The lake's glowing blue algae reflected off the white limestone provided a soft ambient light with no clue as to the sun's position.

Finished, they stood back to admire their work. "Looks plenty sturdy to me," Jim said. "Ready?"

"You bet." Ronnie grinned in anticipation but when he looked back at Eli and Grizzy, his smile left him. "Don't worry. If we find a way out, we'll come back for you."

"Oh, you'll be back. That's for certain," Eli replied.

Jim said nothing and just grabbed their backpacks filled with food and survival gear, then pushed their raft out onto the water. Grizzy growled and whined as they jumped aboard, Jim in front, Ronnie behind at the steering tiller.

"Don't worry, Grizzy. They'll be back like I said. Assumin' they don't drown o'course," Eli said. "We'll be waiting for you right here."

Jim glanced back and saw Eli standing atop the tall boulder on the beach, while Grizzy pawed at the sand. Jim frowned at them both, grabbed his paddle, and dug in sending them out onto the vast smooth lake.

Ronnie did his part on the steering tiller.

Jim grinned back. It felt good to be moving, finally doing something to take control of their fate. The shorelines remained visible on either side, but before them the water stretched far ahead, turning a darker and darker shade of blue in the distance.

"I read somewhere that volcano tunnels can go on for as much as 50 or 60 miles. I sure hope this one doesn't." Said, Ronnie.

"Let's hope not."

"Can't see the bottom anymore. I wonder how deep it gets."

"Pretty deep, I'm guessing." Jim peered down into the clear water, seeing some glassy bug-eyed fish swim by.

"Wow. What are those?"

"I don't know. Something that can live in caves I guess."

"If these fish are here, does it mean they have a way of getting out?"

"That's what we're going to find out."

"Right." Ronnie lashed the tiller and put his back into paddling, his recently earned muscles bulging with effort.

"This is good practice for those rivers we'll have to take to get home," Jim said between breaths as he dug his paddle in deep, rowing in unison with Ronnie. The wide lake eventually narrowed, as the walls of the cavern curved and closed in. The change sparked Jim's memories. "When I was a kid, me and my friends went down the Talkeetna River. It's pretty smooth for the most part, but when the water's high you can hit some rapids in the narrows. Sometimes you have to portage out."

"To what out?"

"Portage. Carry your boat on land past the rough parts."

"Don't think that's an option down here—no room," Ronnie observed, pointing at the walls meeting the water.

"No, but I don't think we have to worry about rapids in here. This water's smooth as silk."

Whenever they stopped talking, the cavern became so eerily quiet, that it felt almost sacrilegious to disturb the silence. For a long while the only sound was the gentle lapping from their paddles as they made their way through winding passage.

In the distance ahead they could see a faint glow of light. The water current seemed to be increasing, speeding the raft ahead. "Oh shit!" Ronnie yelled. "Look at that." A giant whirlpool appeared in the distance, spinning and sucking the water down a huge spiraling maelstrom of death.

"Back paddle" Jim yelled, "faster, harder, we can't slow down...we're going to be sucked into that thing. Hold on."

Suddenly a giant head appeared out of the water, charging against the raft. Its huge back and flippers rose from the water thrashing and crashing like a prehistoric monster. Slowly the raft started moving back away from the whirling water.

The creature continued slowly guiding the raft back to the calm waters of the lake then slowly slid back under the surface.

"What the hell is happening here?" Jim exclaimed. "Am I having a hallucination or did we just get our asses saved by a giant sea serpent?"

"If you're hallucinating then so am I," yelled Ronnie.

The giant head raised next to the raft. Beautiful turquoise green eyes stared at the men from a smooth round face. The eyes seemed to convey peace love and kindness like they had never seen before. The large mouth seemed to slightly turn up in a smile as the creature slowly submerged below the calm water.

"Wow Dude, I feel like I just had an out-of-body experience. Eli will never believe this."

"It saved us from certain death. We better start paddling back to the beach, this is not the way out."

"That was hairy," Ronnie said, and Jim nodded in agreement. "That thing looked like pictures I've seen of Nessie….The Lock Ness monster in Scotland. I guess they never figured out if it's real or not. Well, I believe it. That thing just saved our ass!"

After a long silence, he and Ronnie started paddling again, back the way they'd come. They had no choice but to return to their starting point, which meant searching for another way out, anything but what Eli had advised— to just sit on that beach and wait for their fates to be decided by the whims of a volcanic mountain with the threat of earthquakes or an eruption of molten lava.

Chapter 26
The lake drains

April 4, 1974

Back at the beach, they told Eli the details of being rescued by the lake monster just before almost being sucked into the giant whirlpool. Eli just shook his head in disbelief.

The hours crawled by in a mix of fear and boredom, the ground heaved frequently enough to keep their nerves on edge and disturb any attempt at sleep. On the second day, one of the strongest earthquakes they'd felt to date hit hard, and a sharp cracking sound echoed throughout the cavern. The bear roared and the three men stumbled and fell, unable to maintain their footing.

"Watch it!" Jim yelled and pulled Ronnie aside just as a huge slab of rock and ice crashed down from the cavern ceiling barely missing them both. The deep rumbling slowly faded leaving them shaken but unscathed. Jim let out a sigh of relief and then gaped at what he was seeing now. The lake water was receding.

Jim watched as the water kept retreating, leaving suddenly stranded fish flopping on the sandy bottom, he pictured a giant tub of sloshing water.

"Remember that loud crack, like something big broke? Looks like the earthquake created an opening for the water to escape."

Eli nodded in agreement. "Should we take a look?"

Jim turned to Eli. "You're coming this time?"

Eli shrugged and hefted his rifle. "Water's gone now and I'm curious."

The men and bear trotted down the steps onto the wet sand and out onto the newly revealed lakebed. The strange glassy-looking fish with bulging eyes lay all around gasping for breath. Grizzy ended their suffering by gulping them down.

As the ground sloped downward and they circumvented previously submerged rocks and boulders, the watermarks etched into the rocky sidewalls soon soared above their heads. Looking up at the waterline, Jim estimated they were about 20 feet below what had formerly been the surface, and the sandy floor was still going down. They splashed through puddles where trapped worms wriggled in distress and blue crabs waived their claws threateningly.

There seemed to be a deep trench, like a river that wound through the center of the lakebed. They could see no bottom to the turquoise glowing water. "I sure hope Nessie made it to a safe place in the deep part that won't drain." Said Ronnie.

Jim and Ronnie walked side by side while Eli and the bear trailed behind. Grizzy was gobbling up more thrashing fish making disturbing slobbery crunching sounds.

"Oh man, this is freaking me out," Ronnie said in a low voice.

"Just try to think of it as a gigantic swimming pool... with a leak."

"Sure, except this one's built under a mountain that could blow any minute."

"True." He hadn't forgotten.

Jim glanced back at Eli just in time to see him pick up another dying fish and toss it to Grizzy. The bear caught it in midair and swallowed it whole, smacking it wetly. Jim smiled and turned away.

When the water was ankle-high and getting deeper he came to a stop, hearing a faint but steady roar in the distance. "You hear that?"

Ronnie nodded.

Grizzy stopped eating and lifted his head, sniffing the air, ears listening intently. Grizzy snuffled and snorted, shook his huge head, and took a shuffling step backward.

"Grizzy's sayin' he don't like what's ahead," Eli said.

"Yeah, me either." Jim scowled at the narrowing lakebed before them, the long view now cut off by a curve in the cavern walls where they began to close in. He remembered the whirlpool he and Ronnie encountered when they'd gone through those narrow passages on the raft.

Jim glanced up and around at the exposed sides of the now nearly empty lake. "How about we climb up for a better look?"

Ronnie tilted his head back to look up at the exposed cliff. "Oh man, that's uh… that's pretty steep. Maybe we should go back the way we came and see if we can walk along the edge."

"There wasn't any ledge before. You can see where it starts back there." Jim pointed up and just behind to where the rocky wall gradually grew away from the side of the cavern to form a lip. "Looks wide enough to walk on starting about there."

"Yeah, but that's a long way up," Ronnie countered.

"There's some slope to it and lots of outcroppings. Plenty to grab onto. We'll be fine."

Eli scratched at his beard thoughtfully as he examined the sharply rising terrain. "Hmmm…s'pose it's doable. But only if'n Grizzy agrees." He turned to the bear and gestured at the rock wall. "Whacha think, Griz? Is it a go?"

The bear looked up, snorted, then shuffled over and started to climb. He went up the rock face rapidly, overtaking the rough outcroppings in huge galloping leaps.

"See, it's not so bad," Jim said.

"Sure. Long as you've got four legs with claws attached," Ronnie said.

"Look, there's no shale, no debris rolling off. That's solid footing. You'll be fine."

"When you boys finally get around to convincin' yourselves, I'll see you at the top." Eli slung the ancient rifle over his shoulder, grabbed onto a protruding rock, and started up.

Jim watched Eli's smooth upward progress, demonstrating a physical prowess belying his age. Another indication that Eli was no ordinary man. Jim shook off his discomfort, then gestured at Ronnie. "You're next."

Hesitating for a moment, Ronnie mumbled a series of colorful curses, then grabbed onto the same rock Eli had begun with and pulled himself up. Jim followed right behind planning to arrest Ronnie's fall should he slip. The climb wasn't nearly as easy as Grizzy and Eli had made it look. The rocks were wet and slippery, and far from evenly spaced. It took Jim's total concentration to carefully position each foot before reaching for the next handhold.

Halfway up the wall, Jim heard Ronnie grunt and curse above him.

"You okay?"

"No, man. I'm not okay. I'm stuck."

"Just grab onto the next rock and keep climbing."

"There's nothing here, dude. I'm screwed."

"Hang on." Jim found another toehold and pushed up next to Ronnie. From there he could see the rock face above Ronnie's head was smooth as glass. "Shit."

"Told you."

"To your right, boys!" Eli's voice came from above.

Jim looked up to see Eli grinning down at them and pointing to where rocks jutted out just below and to their right.

"Got it!" Jim yelled back. "We have to go back down a bit," he told Ronnie.

"This is bogus. If I live through this, I'm going to kill you."

"Just keep going."

It took another five minutes of taut nerves and muscular torture to reach the top where Eli waited with an outstretched hand. Jim marveled at the old man's strength as he lifted them effortlessly up and over the edge onto a level berm of what looked like cut granite. They sat there panting, waiting to catch their breath. Eli shook his head and chuckled.

The roar of rushing water ahead echoed off the cavern roof which now was just yards above their heads. The stone ledge followed the top of the lake wall curving ahead and out of sight.

When the others looked at Jim expectantly, he took the lead again. Ronnie followed close behind with Eli and the bear once again at the rear. As they came around the bend, they had a clear view of what remained of the lake below. What had previously been smooth calm water had turned into a winding rushing river.

"Bet yer glad ya ain't still on that raft now," Eli said.

"You got that right! Let's see where this goes." He walked ahead along the ledge as it wound along noting evidence of how much water had been here before and what little of it remained. The walls were about twenty feet apart now and the water level had dropped about 40 feet below the high water marks. The dim cavern grew brighter and brighter as they went. Excited, Jim sped up to see what lay around the next bend, certain to finally find the opening he hoped to let in the light of day.

And there it was, sunlight streaming in through the shattered side of the mountain revealing an open sky of gray filled with smoke and ash. The roaring sound of rushing water grew louder and louder as they slowly crept forward. They came upon a drop-off where the water rushed over the edge creating a waterfall that disappeared in a bluish-white mist. Jim skidded to a halt, the ledge ahead was gone, and the granite path neatly sheared off as if a giant had taken a cleaver to it.

"Woah!" Ronnie exclaimed. "I gotta get a picture."

Jim watched as Ronnie slipped off his backpack, opened it, and pulled out his camera. Dropping to his knees Ronnie focused the lens on the scene below. He held very still and slowly clicked for a long exposure, then carefully replaced the camera in its waterproof bag and put it away before shrugging his pack on again.

"Well guys," Jim said, "Were not getting out through here. That looks to be at least a thousand-foot drop straight down. Without proper climbing gear, there is no way."

Somebody had to have made this, Jim thought, just like those stone steps.

"Whoever built this place must have made another exit. We have to be missing something, a clue, a sign, something. Let's get back to the beach while we still can."

Chapter 27
The Escape

April 5, 1974

It took hours to retrace their route, back along the ledge of the wall until it petered out, then the steep climb down to the exposed lakebed and across the length of it to return to the golden beach and curving stone stairway with the blocked entrance at its top. Grizzy's deep tracks left the wet prints in the lakebed and trailed up the sand.

The ground shook, rocks fell off the walls, and cracks were spreading across the ice ceiling. Dust and smoke filled the air. A loud rumbling like a freight train passing echoed through the cavern then calmed.

Exhausted, the men collapsed onto the beach with their backs against the rock wall.

They had previously searched the entire beachfront and rocky walls but Jim was certain they had missed something. Whoever or whatever had built this place had to have created another exit.

"I've been thinking," Jim said. "I remember in science class at school, we were studying volcanoes. As best as I can remember there's the magma chamber at the bottom and a vent leading through layers of rock to the top, or surface. During an eruption, the lava flows up the main vent spewing out ash, steam, and lava into the atmosphere."

"Thanks for the science class but how does that help our situation." Asked Ronnie.

"I'll tell you how if you let me finish."

"Okay…Okay, go on professor."

"In addition to the main vent, many volcanoes also have secondary vents and tunnels.

Now here's what I think." Jim kneeled on the sand, brushing a flat spot, and began to sketch with his finger. "Consider the cave above…Eli's home, and the tunnels with the hot pools. They all lead down here to this giant cavern. I think those tunnels are volcano vents from an eruption hundreds or thousands of years ago. Above our heads, the ice ceiling was the main vent. When this thing erupted it blew the top of the mountain off sending the lava and ash out the top and through the side vents, one of which is Eli's cave."

"Then how did the ice ceiling and lake get here?" asked Ronnie.

"Probably over the last thousand years, the crater filled up with rain and snow. The heat from the magma below and the steaming hot pools warmed the lake water leaving the ceiling to freeze in the outside elements. Once the lake warmed enough to flow it drained out the mountain side reaching its current level, At least until that last earthquake opened it up and drained."

Looking at Jim's sketch Ronnie commented." Do you mean…..We are standing inside a volcano that's getting ready to erupt. And below our feet is the magma chamber?"

"That's exactly what I mean. Feel how warm the sand is, and when it goes, everything around us is going right through the top of this mountain!"

"Holy Shit! We have to get out of here fast!"

"We only searched when the lake was full. With the water level down we need to look again at the areas previously covered by the lake. There must be a secondary vent, maybe more than one."

"So we may not have much time at all." Said Ronnie.

" That's right...Let's get to it and fast!" Shouted Jim.

"This constant shaking is scaring the shit out of me. Come on Eli we need you and Grizzy to help us look. " Yelled Ronnie as the two men hurried off.

"I reckon I ain't got nothing better to do. Might as well. Come on Grizzy let's have a look."

"I'll take the left side and you guys go down the right. Look for anything, an opening, a crack in the wall, anything." Shouted Jim as he hurried to the opposite wall.

Ronnie and Eli had to hurry around to the opposite side of the subterranean river that had appeared after the lake drained. It seemed to still be flowing with no bottom in sight. Grizzy loped along behind.

Blue tinted Seaweed and kelp hung from the still dripping walls making it difficult to see the rock surface. Algae spread across the rocky floor making it slippery to walk and fields of giant mushrooms sprouted from the cracks. Little crab-like things were scurrying around their feet. Slimy snail-like slugs hung from the rocks. A twelve-inch eel or sea snake shot out of a pool of water making Ronnie almost fall off his feet as he jumped back. "Shit!" he yelled. "This place sucks!"

Jim was having similar problems on the other side as he hurriedly inspected for any possible way out of this underground tomb.

Grizzly suddenly let out a roar and jumped back about five feet as a giant head rose out of the bottomless river water they stood next to. "Damn!" yelled Eli. "It's the monster up and close. I'm getting the hell out of here!" As he spun around sliding and falling into a pile of kelp.

"Wait," Ronnie yelled. "It saved us once. Maybe it's trying to help. "Hey, Jim. "Ronnie yelled. "Over here… Nessie came back to visit."

Jim started running to join them but he was on the opposite side of the river and had to run back and around. "I'm coming as fast as I can."

Grizzy didn't seem to know what to do but stood in front of Eli guarding his lifelong friend.

Nessie was slowly swimming down the river where it came close to the cliffside, looking back as if to make sure they followed.

An outcropping of rocks covered in glowing slimy algae appeared around the next bend. The monster flapped its giant fins splashing waves of water on the rock wall exposing an opening.

"Jim, Jim!" Ronnie screamed. "There's something here….an opening in the rock wall. Nessie led us to a tunnel. It seems to know we're trapped and trying to help."

Jim ran up breathing hard sliding to a stop on the slippery rocks and staring up at the head of this huge creature.

Almost whispering like he didn't want to scare it off Jim said, "I still feel like I'm hallucinating, but if this thing, whatever it is, wants to help, we can sure use it."

The men and bear stood silently staring up at the huge creature from another Millennium, not believing their eyes. Transfixed by the beautiful green eyes that stared hypnotically for a long moment like it was reading their thoughts. It then seemed to smile as the giant head slipped below the surface.

Grizzy let out what sounded like a sigh or whimper, not a growl as the monster slipped away.

The men silently stared at one another mesmerized by what they had just witnessed.

"No one will ever believe this." Said Ronnie. "And I didn't have my camera…..Shit!"

"I saw it and I don't believe it." Said Jim. "Let's go check this tunnel."

They ran up to the opening, parting away the rest of the vegetation finally revealing the entrance to a tunnel.

Grizzy sniffed the foul air, let out a low growl, and backed away from the opening.

"Grizzy don't like that none, Aint sure I do either." Said Eli.

"I think this is the vent tube and the mountain is still shaking. I say we strap on our gear and see where this goes. Hopefully, it's our passage to the outside." Said Jim.

After gathering up their gear Jim lit one of the lemon-scented candles. The sour-sweet fragrance mixed with the smell of foul air and mold.

Jim ducked his head as he went through the opening. Ronnie, Grizzy, and Eli followed. Light from the flickering candle flame danced on the rough stone walls. Jim noted the absence of chisel marks in the rock, clear evidence that this tunnel had not been carved by ancient hands.

The tunnel angled upward its walls glistening wet, and slimy things slithered about. The ceiling, several feet above their heads, still dripped water leaving standing pools on the floor that rippled with things. There was sufficient elbow room on either side even for Grizzy.

As the tunnel climbed above the water line they could see the walls and ceiling were decorated with the same red-pigmented paintings as those in the lake cavern. Further ahead they came to small rooms or side tunnels that had been carved off to the side of the main tunnel. These small rooms were filled with what appeared to be ancient wrapped bodies, their bones visible through rotting cloth. Alongside them were clay pots, beads, and figurines. A burial cave.

"An archaeologist would have a field day in here," Ronnie said.

Grizzy made a low growling sound and backed away. "Grizzy don't like this place." Said Eli backing away with his bear. "I don't much neither."

"This place must be hundreds of years old" Commented Jim. "Ancient native Indian sacred burial grounds. I guess they discovered the vent tunnel and chiseled out burial chambers.

I've heard legends that a place like this existed, but to my knowledge, no one ever knew where it was located. An ancient sacred and secret place. Wow, it really does exist. "

The mountain gave a giant shake knocking the men off their feet, dust stung their eyes and noses as they huddled on the floor covering their heads from falling debris.

"The shaking seems to be getting stronger and more frequent." Said Jim, "We need to keep moving while we still can. Let's go! NOW!"

They had been moving through the tunnel for what seemed hours, having to stop and clear rock slides and boulders from their path, stopping to cover up each time the shaking came again. Then Ronnie yelled, "Look ahead." A dim light was barely visible in the distance. Could this be an opening to the outside world? The light at the end of the tunnel....Finally.

The shaking started like never before......Rocks, sand, and debris were falling from above trying to close the tunnel. "RUN" Jim Screamed as they all scrambled for the opening.....Dust obscured their vision as they ran toward the light.

Then the light went out!

Chapter 28
Out of the mountain

April 5, 1974

Jim imagined he was coming back from a nightmare as rough hands shook him back to awareness. He was half covered in rocks and debris and Eli was vigorously shaking him. Ronnie sat beside him holding a candle. "Wake up Jim! Eli shouted, "You okay? Man, you've been out for a while and that's quite a knot on your head."

"Oh shit! What happened….Are we out?"

"That last quake caused a cave-in and the ceiling came down right on your head. Are you alright? Feeling okay?" asked Ronnie.

"Yeah, I think I'm okay. I've Got a trophy headache and my vision's a bit fuzzy, but I don't think anything is broken. Are you guys Okay?"

"We're all right but the tunnel caved in on both sides of us. We're trapped. Can't go ahead or back. This truly sucks!"

Jim was staring at Ronnie's candle with a dazed look in his eyes," Look at your candle Ronnie. The flame…It's flickering. There's a draft….airflow. We must be close to the exit. Let's start digging. Eli, get that bear of yours upfront and tell him to dig us out. That's what bears do, isn't it? Come on Grizzy dig us out of here!"

Grizzy squeezed past the men and started digging, his giant claws plowing into the rubble that was blocking their exit, sending rocks, dust, and debris over the men behind him.

A sliver of light appeared through the dust that filled the air. This seemed to encourage the bear to dig with even more gusto.

Everyone jumped in scratching and pulling everything to the rear as the opening grew larger.

"You go Grizz!" Yelled Ronnie, as they all laughed at being freed.

They crawled from the tunnel onto a ledge that was almost as big as a football field. The ledge was set back under an overhanging rock ceiling. They greedily breathed in the slightly smokey fresh air, coughing and wheezing as they gazed over the stunning view of the snow-covered Talkeetna mountain range in the distance.

"Holy crap!" shouted Ronnie, "Look back here."

The cliffside wall behind them had been carved into a stone city. There must have been hundreds of rooms several stories high covering the entire face of the cliffside.

They stood before this ancient city astonished by the craftsmanship. Decorative stone pillars stood before what appeared to be a main entranceway, and broken bits of pottery littered the ground. A narrow trail led along the cliffside in both directions. The trail appeared to have been well traveled by the former residents, whoever they were, and worn deep, but still looked in relatively good condition, considering it certainly hadn't been used in a very long time.

"Cliff dwellings." Said Jim. " I've never known of any in Alaska." This place must date back thousands of years to when the Alaska temperature was much warmer. To my knowledge, no one knows this place exists"

" I have got to get pictures of this." Said Ronnie as he dug for his camera.

"I wish we had time to explore this place, it looks fascinating. But this mountain is likely to blow at any minute and we need to keep moving." Jim hurriedly said, "Eli, I think this is the backside of the mountain surrounding your valley. It looks like the trail leads back in that direction." Pointing to his left. "and that direction goes towards Talkeetna."

"Well then, I reckon now is where we part company. Me and Grizzy have to get back to our home, or what's left of it? It's been a real pleasure havin you boys around, and I think even Grizzy has takin a liken to ya."

Eli gathered them both in a huge bear hug and Grizzy made a low whimpering sound.

Jim and Ronnie hugged him back, fighting back the tears

Hope you boys make it outa here and get back to your families real soon." Said Eli, as he and his bear headed off down the trail.

" I understand why you can't leave here. You saved our lives and we won't ever forget it." Jim shouted as Eli and Grizzy ambled off.

"Later Eli, take care." Said, Ronnie

Ronnie and Jim were standing near the trailhead while Ronnie was trying to focus his camera, when another rumble and giant shake hit, and the ledge they were standing on began crumbling beneath their feet sending them tumbling down the mountainside, sliding with boulders, trees, and rubble down they went.

Sliding and rolling end over end they finally came to rest on the canyon floor.

"Holy crap!" Shouted Ronnie, "Will this never end?"

They climbed back to their feet, coughing, spitting, and shaking the dust and debris from their torn and dirty clothes. Miraculously they sustained only minor cuts and bruises.

The mountain was erupting. Sending up smoke, ash, rocks, and debris thousands of feet in the air blocking the sun and turning the day into night.

Go-Go! shouted Jim, "We have to get some distance from this thing!"

"They both began to stumble and run, choking and coughing on the foul air, eyes burning and blurring their vision.

They ran and ran, jumping over fallen trees and rocks and dodging flying objects until finally collapsing to the ground. Total exhaustion brought them down. They had to rest.

"Do you think they made it?" Ronnie breathlessly asked while gasping for air.

"I sure hope so. And I hope we make it!"

As soon as they could move on they pushed as hard as they could. Stumbling and falling, but rushing on, knowing they had to get away while still trying to find the river. The sky grew darker with smoke, ash, and falling debris. The ground continued to shake. Fissures were opening at their feet causing rivers of dirt to cave underground as they dodged and jumped to safety.

"Oh, man!" Shouted Ronnie, "This is scaring the shit out of me. I don't know how much more I can take."

"Suck it up! We are not giving up. Even if I have to drag your ass out!"

"Okay dude, you don't have to get nasty."

Day and night they pushed on, ever looking for the big river. Stopping only for short rest breaks and a quick bite of dried food, they kept going. They didn't even know how many days and nights they had been on the run, only that they were completely exhausted and about ready to collapse. The mountain behind them smoked and shuddered, a red stream of lava flowing down one side.

"There," shouted Jim, "the river, it's flowing. The quake, the eruption, and the lava flow must have broken the glacier ice. Let's go, buddy, we have a raft to build—ASAP."

With renewed energy and an adrenalin rush from finding the river, they somehow raced on.

Hours later using Eli's old tools they had chopped and sawn pieces of the downed trees and strapped them together with rawhide ties, building a very rough but hopefully seaworthy raft.

Jim gazed at the rushing river saying "Okay old buddy, this is it. It's going to be a rough ride but it's our only way out. Are you ready for this? Once we're on that river all we can do is hang on."

"I am so ready! I hope this thing holds together. Let's do this."

They dragged the raft to the raging river and jumped aboard as they pushed off! The river was rushing down fast and carried mud, trees, dead animals, and everything else along with it. Racing downstream at breakneck speed, they encountered more boulders and uprooted trees, dead animals, and rocks. They had no way to steer but hung on, gaining distance. Behind them, the mountain blew again with a huge roar, debris, and ash flying thousands of feet into the air. Red angry lava spewed from the top. The already swollen river suddenly surged ahead as a tidal wave of water, debris, trees, and boulders roared down upon them. Riding the maelstrom, all they could do was hang on. A huge crest lifted the raft as high as the trees still standing at the side of the river and threw it sideways into a giant tree where it snagged in its branches. The tidal wave left them behind and the water receded, leaving them high and dry, caught in the treetop twenty feet above the ground. They were alive, and still had their gear tightly strapped to the raft—but they were twenty feet in the air, stuck in a tree clinging on with their hands and knees.

"Man, no one's ever gonna believe this," Ronnie said as he peered over the edge to the ground below," but what an awesome ride that was…Wow, what a wave!"

Chapter 29
On the River

April 8, 1974

"This is Anchorage news with a breaking story. Mount Sustina in the Talkeetna mountain range has erupted. Smoke and ash have blanketed the area up to twenty thousand feet. All flights have been diverted from Anchorage due to the ash cloud. This is one of the most remote areas of the Talkeetna mountain range with no reported habitation in the area. More news to follow."

***

Jim and Ronnie watched below them as the river surged and rose again to carry huge boulders and trees with it. The raft seemed safe above the raging torrent until the tree supporting it trembled as the violent water washed out the shoreline, toppling the tree and raft back into the onslaught of rampant water and debris.

"Hold on!" shouted Jim, "We're going for another river ride."

"Oh, shit, I'm not ready for this," yelled Ron, holding on with all his strength.

The raft slapped down into the water, somehow staying upright as it spun in the rapids. Again they were at the mercy of the river, cascading down the valley at breakneck speed, struggling to hold on to the raft. To fall off was to die.

On and on they raced, and the raft was starting to come apart. The rawhide bindings stretched, loosened by the water and from the hits it took.

"Don't know how long we can ride this thing," yelled Jim. " It's starting to come apart. Get your pack and gear strapped on. We may have to jump clear ."

"Okay," Ron shouted over the roar of water. "Man, I sure wish I had a life jacket."

The valley widened and the river slowed some and became more shallow. The raft stabilized enough for them to pull it back together and twist the rawhide to keep it tight. it seemed to be working, the logs held together. Jim let out a deep breath in relief. "It looks like we're going to make it. We can just kick back and relax until we get to Talkeetna."

They slowly drifted down the river. Feeling as though they were finally out of danger they started to relax. Drifting around the next bend they heard the roar before they saw the source. A cascading waterfall dropping hundreds of feet was coming up in front of them. Rocks, boulders, trees, and debris gushed over the falls and out of sight.

"Oh, shit Jump!" Jim shouted. "We'll never make it through that."

They leaped towards the shoreline, Ronnie's pack was torn from his back as he hit the forceful water. Jim, right behind him, grabbed branches along the riverside and reached out to Ronnie, pulling him along with him, grabbing anything to hold them. They were holding on with all their strength fighting the rapid current, being drug under and spitting water before finally being able to struggle to shore.

***

Karen and Pattie anxiously sat in Karen's living room watching the news.

"They're going to have lots of airplanes over that area reporting on the volcano eruption," said Karen. "Maybe there's a chance they'll spot the guys."

"Why do you do this?" cried Pattie, "They're gone. Can't you accept that?"

"No!" shouted Karen, "we can't give up hope. They will make it back. I know they will."

"I wish I could believe that. It's been months. How could they possibly be alive?"

"I can't explain it," said Karen, "I just know they'll be home soon."

***

"Wow!" said Ronnie. "That was some roller coaster ride. Not sure I want to do that again."

"Amen brother that was quite a ride. Now, all we have to worry about is getting the rest of the way out of here. We made some good distance. I figure the river must have been rushing at twenty to thirty miles an hour. We were on the raft for about five hours, so we must have traveled for one to two hundred miles. From now on we walk! Let's take a break and check our resources. I have my pack, supplies, and the forty-four mag.

"Sorry I lost my pack in the river," said Ronnie. "It just ripped off my back."

"No worries, at least we both made it out alive. It was getting a bit iffy there for a while. We have plenty in my pack.

"Yeah, but my camera was in that pack. How will we ever convince anyone to believe our story? I know I wouldn't believe it."

They checked out their remaining gear and had some dried jerky as they looked around in horror at the surreal landscape.

The sky was dark with volcanic ash blocking out the sun. It looked like the aftermath of Armageddon— huge trees lay rooted from the ground, giant boulders were scattered around like toys and swelling carcasses of moose and caribou lay still in the endless mud, legs sticking up as if reaching for the sky. The air, permeated with volcanic smoke, watered their eyes. Grit entered their mouth and nostrils with each breath, requiring them to tie bandanas around their faces.

They had lost the ax and saw, so another raft was out of the question. "Well, old buddy, I guess we better start walking," said Jim. It's going to be a bitch maneuvering around all the crap scattered everywhere. At least the tidal wave took away all the snow and ice, and most of the brush along the riverside."

"I'm ready Dude. Want me to carry the pack for a while?"

"I got it, you can take over later, let's go."

They started off walking down the river, the mud sucking at their feet, knowing this direction had to eventually lead out of the mountains.

"Do you think they'll send aircraft up here to check out the eruption?" asked Ronnie.

"Don't know, man. They might wait a few days until the smoke settles. That stuff's hard on aircraft engines. Some of the crazy talking heads from the TV news might talk someone into flying out here to get a video of the eruption site. We should keep our eyes and ears open in case someone does fly by."

They walked for hours until darkness enveloped the landscape, forcing them to find shelter in a tangle of rooted-out trees and boulders. Exhausted from their ordeal and unable to start a fire to ward off the cold creeping in with the darkness. they slumped behind the tree eating dried jerky with dirty river water from the canteen as the cold enveloped them like a shroud.

"Just think of what we have experienced," said Jim, "Weathered in for days at a remote lake that few people even know about. We spent months in a volcanic cave with a 125-year-old Civil War vet and found more gold than we could carry, came face to face with an extinct sea monster, and lived with a Grizzly bear. We escaped a volcano eruption discovered an ancient cliff dwelling that no one knows is there, and rode a tidal wave down the river on a log raft. What an experience, once in a lifetime! I have a feeling we still have more fun to look forward to."

Waking from a fitful, cold sleep they faced another dismal day—the bleak ruined landscape displayed by sunlight filtered through volcanic ash cast surreal shadows from the scattered debris.

After a quick bite of jerky washed down with muddy river water, they pressed on, staggering with the mud sucking at their feet. Moving with a purpose—get out, find someone…anyone!

They saw animals at a distance: a bear that suddenly got their scent and crashed off into the brush, several moose that paid them no attention, and a lone wolf that followed them through the day before wandering off.

Day after day they trudged on, exhausted, on they walked—downstream, always downstream.

The days seemed to be getting brighter as the ash dissipated with the arctic winds.

On the tenth day, they heard an airplane flying overhead. They jumped and shouted and waved their arms in frustration as the plane shot by taking no notice of the two men below.

"Shit!" Ronnie shouted, "Asshole! You could have looked down."

"We're hard to see down here. They're going to get a look at the volcano," said Jim. "Let's get going."

The following day as they rounded a bend in the river they came to a lake, cluttered with floating debris. It looked to be a few miles across and a log lodge stood on the far shore.

"Look!" Jim shouted. "We made it. A lodge, civilization, and people. What a beautiful sight! Let's go, partner looks like we're home free."

Chapter 30
The Lodge

April 18, 1974

The lodge was further than they thought and the trekking was hard…stumbling through chest-high Alders and the constant sucking mud it was early evening when they finally reached the lodge. Staggering up the porch steps they rushed into the building. "Hello, hello, anybody home?" Jim yelled. "Where is everyone, HELLO?" he shouted again.

"Hey, anybody here?" Ron yelled. "Shit Dude there's nobody here."

They ran through the rooms looking for anyone, finding no one.

The lodge was beautifully constructed of varnished white pine, two stories with bedrooms upstairs. Rustic furniture filled the rooms and fishing/hunting pictures decorated the walls. It was a fly-in hunting/fishing lodge. A layer of dust and grit covered everything indicating no one had been there for a while.

Ronnie went directly to the kitchen finding the cabinets were stocked with canned goods. Real food. Beans, stew, soup, Spam, and coffee. "Oh, Dude, food….and coffee! I have to have coffee."

"Go for it." said Jim, "There's plenty of firewood and they probably have a well here somewhere with fresh water. Then we can eat. I'm starved!"

They found the hand pump in the front yard and washed off the grit and mud from their journey. Laughing they joyfully threw water at each other as they drank the pure clear well water and poured buckets over their heads.

"Let's brew up a pot of coffee and maybe some beef stew. I've had enough jerky to last a lifetime.

After a delicious meal of store-bought food, beef stew, beans, crackers, and coffee, they relaxed on the front porch sipping wine they had found." This wine is so good." Commented Ronnie. "Civilization at last!."

They discussed their current circumstances and what they should do next.

"What now Jim? We have shelter and food, but we're still not home."

"I know. This lodge was certainly accessed by floatplanes, but there's no way a floatplane can land on that lake now with all the crap floating on the water. We'll think of something, but right now after the hot food and wine, I can hardly think straight or keep my eyes open. Let's crash for the night and come up with a plan in the morning."

"Okay, but please don't use that term. One crash is enough."

"Sorry, I'm going to pick a room and cr…..uh, get some sleep."

"I sure hope Eli and Grizzy made it out."

" Yeah, I do too. We owe our lives to them. Good night."

"Night"

The next morning after a great night's sleep on real mattresses they filled up on oatmeal and coffee as they discussed their options.

"So, no floatplane can land on the lake and no wheel plane can land on the beach. Looks like our ride out will have to be a chopper," said Jim.

"I agree, so how do we lure one in here to pick us up?"

"I've been thinking about that, come with me."

They walked down to the beach that was covered with debris, logs, boulders, and brush.

"We need a distress sign that can be seen from a distance," said Jim.

" With all this shit on the beach, how're we gonna do that?"

"We have to clear an area of the beach large enough for a big SOS, then scrounge around the lodge to see what we can use to spell it out so it can't be missed. We'll need to stack a bunch of the logs and brush in a big pile for a bonfire to light when the next plane flies over. We'd better get scrounging!"

"Let's do it"

They started searching through the rooms urgently looking for anything that might work for their SOS message, finding white bed sheets that should be visible on the dark sandy beach.

"There must be a tool shed around here somewhere for keeping this place up. Let's look around back." Said Jim.

Behind the lodge, they couldn't believe their luck when they found an outbuilding that stored a four-wheel-drive quad, portable generator, block and tackle, and five jerry cans of gasoline in addition to rakes, shovels, picks, and various other tools.

"Bitchin', Dude, a four-wheel-drive quad! I used to have one just like this. If we can get this thing running we can use it to clear the beach and the extra gas for the bonfire."

"Let's see if it'll start, maybe we can clear enough beach for a bush plane to land. Probably only need about six hundred feet."

Ronnie jumped on the quad, checked the fuel level, and pulled the starter rope. The engine fired up on the second pull. They high-fived each other and laughed out loud as Ronnie drove to the beach.

The quad had a blade on the front which was just the thing for clearing the beach. Ronnie pushed the debris into one big pile for the bonfire. Larger stumps were winched out with the block and tackle.

Several planes flew overhead in the distance—too far away to signal. It took them several more days of hard work but they finally managed to clear a stretch of beach twenty feet wide by six hundred feet long. They had built the stack of firewood five feet high and had cans of gas ready close by.

To make their help message, they laid out logs wrapped in the white bedsheets from the lodge to spell out the word SOS, in 60-foot-long letters, along with their downed plane's number 'N1659R'. If any pilot saw that sign, they'd know who was there and why.

They planned to continue extending the runway until help arrived.

On day eight, right around noon while Jim and Ron were inside eating lunch, a de Havilland Beaver on floats made a low pass over the lodge. When they heard the roar of its big radial engine zoom overhead they knocked over bowls and chairs in the way as they ran outside, waving and shouting as the Beaver came back around, rocking its wings to signal they'd been seen.

Circling back around once more, the pilot dropped a plastic water bottle with a note inside— "Saw your SOS and N1659R—glad you found my place—will send help."

***

April 21, 1974

"Karen, This is Ted at flight service. I know we haven't talked in a while but I have news."

Karen waited in dread for the announcement they had found the bodies of their husbands.

"Karen, they've been found! At least we think it's them. A bush pilot was flying out to check on his fishing lodge in the Talkeetna mountains and found SOS and N5169R spelled out on the beach at his lodge. Your husband's plane number. The pilot said he saw two men on the beach waving"

Karen almost fainted and lost her balance, tears streaming down her face and she sobbed.

"Thank God! I knew they were alive. Why didn't the guy land and pick them up?"

"He was in a float plane and the lake at the lodge was too full of logs and debris to land.

We hope to get a helicopter out there at first light. Sounds like they've got a nice lodge to stay in until we get there."

"Thank you, Ted!, Oh God! I can't believe it. I'm shaking all over. I have to go now and call Pattie. Please call me as soon as you know anything."

"Will do, by for now."

Karen couldn't call Pattie fast enough!

"Pattie, they found them and they're alive."

"Where, how, when, tell me! Pattie sobbed through tears of joy.

"A remote fishing lodge in the Talkeetna mountains. There was a distress message on the beach saying, SOS and N5169R, Jim's plane number. And the guys ran out waving at the plane as it flew over."

"I can't believe it, after all these months. What they must have gone through. Thank God they're safe."

" They hope to send a helicopter out in the morning."

***

Ronnie grabbed Jim in a bear hug. "Dude, we did it! They saw us. We're being rescued."

Laughing, the pair jumped up and down, pumping fists in the air, screaming and hollering. "Home! Home! Whoohoo! We're going home!"

Out of breath but grinning still, Ronnie bent over with his hands pressed on his thighs. "Oh man, I can't wait to see Pattie."

"Yeah, yeah, it'll be great. Ha, you know, they probably won't even recognize us."

"You're right. Think we should shave?" Ronnie straightened and fingered the golden ruff covering his cheeks and chin.

They shared a look, then smiled. "Nah."

"So um, how long do you think it'll take for rescue to come for us?"

Jim considered the question and the time of day. "Tomorrow, I'd guess. Probably first thing in the morning, if it were me in charge."

"I wasn't going to tell you, but I found a bottle of Jack Daniels in the kitchen with the wine." said Ronnie, "I was going to save it for just this occasion."

"Let's do it. We deserve a drink after all we've been through."

That evening as the twilight was growing to dusk, they splurged, eating everything left in the cupboards for their last meal out here, then sat on the porch—truly happy and full for the first time in months—celebrating their imminent rescue. Ronnie ceremoniously opened the bottle of whisky and poured its amber liquid into two shot glasses.

"A toast," he said, "to whoever owns this lodge and flies that Beaver... Thank you very much for the soft beds and hot food."

"Absolutely. And to Eli and Grizzy. Without them, we never would have made it."

"Maybe not. Hope they made it too. Here's to survival. Ours and theirs."

"And to whoever's going to fly out tomorrow to pick us up."

Each time they raised their glasses and drank to the ones mentioned.

"They toasted their wives, who must have been notified by now of them having been located. It was such a relief to be found and that their hardships were almost over, they toasted everything and were getting a bit tipsy.

They laughed and joked about how their wives probably wouldn't recognize them when Ronnie got a sober look on his face, "Hey Jim, did you just feel something?"

"Like what?" Said Jim still laughing.

Just then a giant tremor shook the ground, almost knocking them off their seats.

"THAT!" Yelled Ronnie.

Chapter 31
Escape from the Lodge

April 28, 1974

"Shit! I guess the volcano wasn't done yet. I hate it when that happens!"Jim yelled.

A tremor shook the ground, almost knocking over their chairs.

They jumped to their feet as the rumbling grew louder, turning into a roar, and they could feel the patio and lodge all around them vibrating like a washing machine with an uneven load. The shaking didn't stop and the planks of the wooden porch started to split. Jim and Ronnie both instinctively looked in the direction of the mountain that had nearly claimed their lives. Then it blew up, an ear-splitting explosion as if a bomb went off. Rocks, smoke, and molten lava shot high into the air, lighting up the night like a red sun. Lightning stabbed downward and it began to rain, soft at first, then harder and harder. Soon the ash-filled water was coming down in sheets so fast and furious it was hard to see even a few feet ahead.

The ground kept shaking and fissures cracked open on the beachfront. Water rolled ashore swallowing up their sheet-wrapped logs that spelled 'SOS'.

"Oh no. No, no, no!" Struggling to stay on his feet and totally sober now, Jim yelled to be heard over the noise, "We have to get out of here. Get the quad and extra gas cans. I'll meet you out back."

Jim ran inside the lodge to grab their backpack, questioning that choice even as he did so, but he knew their ultimate survival depended on it. The entire lodge was rolling and overhead log beams were starting to splinter. He feared it could collapse any moment so he wasted no time as he snatched up his pack, stuffed it with what was left of the food, and rushed back out just as Ronnie came barreling up on the quad.

The rising water was already ankle-deep when Jim jumped on the back and shouted, "Go-go-go!" Ronnie hit the gas, heading for high ground in the foothills, but the flash flood chased them and water was soon lapping at their tires.

"Faster," Jim shouted, "The water's catching up."

"Okay, hang on. This is going to get bumpy. I can hardly see ahead with all the ash and crap in the air." Ronnie shouted. The quad's motor screamed as Ronnie pushed it to the limit, jumping rocks and fallen trees. Jim gasped, straining to see ahead through the dim glow of the headlights. He held tight to Ronnie and the pack as they flew through the air. His life was now in Ronnie's hands, he'd never felt so out of control. The terrain grew even steeper but the four-wheeler kept climbing, doing just what it was designed to do. With no clear destination and the need to climb to safety in his mind, Ronnie kept going up. The foothills became mountains, covered with loose granite and shale. Above the tree line now, even the four-wheel-drive could climb no further. When the tires spun free in the loose shale, he parked at an angle to the slope and shut off the engine.

"Okay. I think we're high enough now."

Jim looked back and released his death grip on Ronnie's waist. He looked down the hill, not able to see very far, but not

seeing any water below. "I think we're clear of the flood water."
"Yeah, I'd say so."

"Man that was one hell of an eruption. I can't believe how fast the lake came up."

"I've seen it happen before. Flash floods like that are killers."

"And just when we were almost home. So what the hell do we do now?"

"Not sure yet, but at least they know where we were."

"Yeah, which means they'll think we drowned down there. Oh man, this is so freakin messed up."

"Come on. We're okay. This isn't the end. We've had way worse than this, and always made it out."

"Right. We could build another bonfire, but Dude, everything's drenched. It could take days, weeks maybe for all this to dry out."

"Plus no one can fly now with that volcano going off again. Not with all that new ash in the air."

"Point taken. So do we hang around here till then or head west again? What do you think makes more sense?"

"I don't know. Just give me a minute to think," Jim struggled to maintain his reasonable calm voice, the one that exuded confidence, but then he just lost it. "God dammit! I can't believe this shit! It's like the whole damn world is out to get us."

Ronnie twisted around to look at him like he was a stranger.

"Sorry. It's just that we were so damn close, and now we're back to square one."

"Yeah, Dude, that's exactly what I was saying, but you said, we'll figure things out. I believe you. We'll figure it out. The ones I feel sorry for are Pattie and Karen. Just when we got their hopes up, they're going to get some really bad news again."

"Okay, I can't see shit in this dark so I say we shelter here for the night and see what we see in the morning."

Chapter 32
Lost

April 28, 1974

Manhandling the heavy Quad across the face of the steep granite hillside was an arduous task. Slipping and sliding, trying to use the engine power and muscle power to horse the machine across the precipitous slope without it tumbling back down the hillside. They finally were able to reach an outcropping of rocks that provided a level space as both men dropped to their knees, sweating and panting from the extreme exertion. They found a suitable rock overhang that provided shelter for the night, if it was even night the sky was so dark from the volcanic ash covering the sun. They kept their bandanas tightly wrapped around their mouth and nose, trying to keep the ash from their eyes. They just needed to stay sheltered until it was safe to continue.

"I have no clue where we are, or even what direction is what. I can't even tell which direction the river is flowing now that it's a giant lake!" Yelled Jim in frustration," Plus it's so damn smokey I can't see fifty feet. Shit, which way do we go? Flip a coin?"

"I don't have a coin," Ronnie replied.

"We have fresh supplies and extra gas so we're not in any immediate danger. Let's try to get some sleep and see what we can figure out in the morning."

They tossed, turned, and shivered, through the cold restless night waking to a grim gray smokey landscape.

The sky started to lighten some and the visibility improved to several hundred yards. There appeared to be several canyons that would lead them downhill, in what direction they didn't know. They just had to try something! Whatever direction, they couldn't just sit there.

They rode the quad for the next few days, exploring several canyons that led to impassible dead ends, always returning to their rock overhang shelter at night, if only to give them a starting reference as to which directions they had already explored. On the afternoon of the fifth day, the quad ran out of gas.

"Well old buddy," said Jim, "Looks like we start walking again. We could wander around in the maze of canyons for the rest of our lives…literally. Pick a direction we haven't already checked out."

After wandering for two more days, exploring even the smallest canyons and faint animal trails they were still lost. It was like a giant maze, twisting and turning with no way out. The smoke, although somewhat cleared still blocked any reference to the stars for help in finding their position.

Running low on supplies the last few days they had been rationing and both men were hungry, exhausted, and foot weary from the constant exertion and depressed to the point of just giving up. They sat down on a rock face not knowing what to do next when Ronnie said" Jim, you ain't gonna believe this, but look over there," pointing back the way they had just come.

"Holy crap!" exclaimed Jim, "is that Grizzy?"

"It sure looks like him, but we had better be ready to run just in case."

The bear slowly walked up to Jim and Ronnie, making its familiar growls and nudging against them for a rub.

"It's Grizzy. He survived and somehow tracked us down," said Jim.

"Or he's been following us this whole time." Said Ronnie.

"I don't see Eli. I sure hope he's okay."

" I do too. It's just like him to figure we were lost and send his bear to help."

"Maybe Grizzy can lead us out of here?" said Ronnie," Hey Grizzy, can you show us the way out?" Grizzy shook his head as if understanding turned around, and started walking away.

"What are we waiting for," yelled Jim, "I will follow that bear anywhere. Come on."

Grizzy led them in directions they would never have considered as if he knew exactly where they needed to go. They walked for days, stopping for rest and sleep at night. Grizzy wandered off each night supposedly to find his dinner, but always returned before first light.

Grizzy meandered along at his bear-like rambling pace, occasionally standing tall on his hind legs, smelling the air, grunting then moving on again. Sometimes, after sniffing the air he would shake his huge head, growl, and alter his course before setting off again. From the break of day until darkness, the men followed him for five days.

On the fifth day, Grizzy slowed to a stop, sat down, and staring off in the distance he grunted in his friendly bear way.

"What's wrong Grizzy? Why are you stopping, there's still lots of daylight left."

"Jim," Ronnie exclaimed while pointing forward. A town, with red roofs partially covered under layers of volcanic ash was visible in the distance. "I think it's Talkeetna! Grizzy did it...He knew! He led us to safety."

The men staggered to a nearby hill, climbing to the top for a better view. "That's Talkeetna all right," Jim exclaimed, " We made it out in one piece."

They turned around and Grizzy was gone. Was he ever really there?

Epilogue

May 6, 1974

They sat around the living room of Jim and Karen's house. A pot of coffee on the table;

Karen and Pattie, are now the best of friends.

Jim and Ronnie were much leaner and fit now with neatly trimmed beards.

Jamie, was taller now, with an air of maturity beyond his years.

Old Red, now clean-shaven and well-dressed in jeans and a flannel shirt and sober.

Jim and Ronnie had been flown home from Talkeetna the previous day, dirty smelly, and exhausted. They had agreed to all meet together the following day for the guys to tell the story of their amazing survival.

The room went silent as Jim and Ronnie lay two beautiful golden bears, a rawhide pouch of golden bullets, and a pouch of gold nuggets on the coffee table.

Jim was the first to speak, "You are not going to believe this!"

***

June 1, 1974

The old man and the bear stood on the mountaintop surveying the valley below that had been their home.

The once-serene valley had been devastated by earthquakes and volcanic eruptions. The valley floor was unrecognizable, being covered with huge boulders that had broken off from the Cliffside above and uprooted trees, brush, and volcanic ash that now littered the valley floor.

They carefully worked themselves down to the valley floor and walked through the desolation that once was pristine and beautiful.

The bear sniffed the air and let out a low growl.

The old man walked slowly as he had been feeling sickly recently and didn't have much energy. He carried the big flintlock rifle over one shoulder.

The door to the cave lay in splinters and the entrance was mostly caved in.

The stream running through the valley floor still flowed, although hampered by the rubble, and steam still rose from the surface.

As the old man looked around with sadness he noticed something in the volcanic ash below his feet that put a smile on his face......a sprout. ...a sprout of a lemon tree!

About the author

Lynn Wyatt worked for Flying Tiger Airlines as an aircraft mechanic and engineer in LAX and in Anchorage where he also flew as a bush pilot for twelve years in single and multi-engine land and seaplanes.

He then worked for United Technologies as an aerospace engineer until his retirement when he became a flight instructor at Gillespie Field.

His ratings include ATP (Airline Transport Pilot), SEL (Single engine land), SES (Single engine Sea), MEL (Multi-Engine Land), MES (Multi Engine Sea), AGI (Advanced Ground Instructor), CFI (Certified Flight Instructor) A&P (Airframe and Powerplant Mechanic.)

Lynn currently lives in Northern Idaho with his wife Mendi in the forest overlooking Lake Pend Oreille.

Lynn is also the author of "Memories from my log book, A Bush Pilot's Story"

Lynn Wyatt

Acknowledgments

Thank you to Marla Anderson for helping me out of my writer's block and getting me back to complete this book.

Thank you to my friends and family who have always encouraged me to write and share more about the times and tales that relate to my previous life experiences.